THE CRYSTAL IN

THE PEACOCK
DIARIES

BOOK 5

Renée Hand

NORTH STAR PRESS OF ST. CLOUD, INC.

St. Cloud, Minnesota

Cover Art and title page by Alla Dubrovich
Text Illustrations by Kaitlin Brown

First Edition: September 2011

ISBN-10: 0-87839-566-0
ISBN-13: 978-0-87839-566-8

Printed in the United States of America.

Published by
North Star Press of St. Cloud, Inc.
P.O. Box 451
St. Cloud, Minnesota 56302
northstarpress.com

Dedication

As always, I wish to thank my family and friends for helping make my dreams a reality. I also wish to thank Jack Metzger. He contributed his character, Steven Einsburg, to this book. I would also like to thank Kaitlin Brown for taking the time to create the inside illustrations. Thank you to all!

A Note to the Readers

You will be learning something new in this case. I will be teaching you about a new cipher. In the past four books we have been learning and practicing a Substitution cipher. This book, and the next five, will contain an Ottendorf cipher. Ottendorf ciphers are book ciphers. Just like book one of this series The Case of the Missing Sock, I will walk you through on how to use a book cipher and it will be explained in detail. I recommend that you follow along, take notes and practice decoding. You should be able to get exactly what I do. If you don't, try again. It's a fairly easy cipher to learn. Below is the cipher key you will be using to solve the cryptograms.

A	B	C	D	E	F	G	H	I	J	K	L	M	N	O	P	Q	R	S	T	U	V	W	X	Y	Z
G	Z	Y	R	Q	V	F	K	W	P	N	A	U	X	H	I	L	E	M	C	B	T	D	J	O	S

Remember to write the cipher key down as well as the cryptograms so you can solve them on a separate piece of paper. I hope you enjoyed Book 4 and your adventure to Pisa, Italy. There was certainly much to learn. This adventure is going to take you to England, where you will be visiting some very scenic and wondrous places with lots of history to share. I hope you have fun and are enjoying the series. As for us, the game is afoot and the Crypto-Capers love a good mystery. I hope you do, too. Good luck!

Renee Hand
www.reneeahand.com

PRELUDE

LIGHTENING CRACKED AS THE EARTH echoed and shook from the roaring thunder. Wind whipped trees, sending branches to the forest floor. Waves pounded the shore of the island. A mansion, strategically placed in the middle of the island, encircled with densely packed trees, was hidden in a layer of darkness and storm. The island had no roads or even cars, but it did have a small circle of green where the trees did not grow. To say the island was secluded was an understatement. There was no other island like this one, or any with the same dangers. In the eeriness of a stormy night the lights of one room popped on, creating a toothless grin on the face of the mansion.

That one room stood out in the gloom, one room that seemed to contain any hope and life. A light shown through those double windows, but as they were covered by a thin curtain, nothing within was revealed. Still the glowing light shined like a beacon in the inky night. Every other window in the house appeared draped in darkness—no light—as if the owner were hiding from the world. The mansion was an interesting place indeed, but it was nothing like the man who dwelled within.

Within that one lighted room, an elderly man with wild white hair, brilliant blue eyes, and black spectacles sat hunched over a magnificent mahogany roll top desk. He ignored the brutal storm that raged outside, though rain beat against the windows and the wind howled. More lightning flashed and thunder shook the house like an earthquake as he finished signing his name to the letter he had been writing. He then pulled out a beige envelope from one of the desk's many little drawers, tossing it on the desk top. The letter was crisp in his hand as he began to fold the paper, tucking it neatly inside of the envelope. With beautiful flare, he wrote a name on the front of the envelope. From another drawer, he lifted a stick of crimson wax and raised it over the flame of the candle on the desk, rotating it in the flame until it softened. He smeared wax onto the envelope edge, sealing it. After setting down the wax stick in its box, he lifted a stamp and pressed it onto the hot wax, holding it there for several seconds. When he lifted the stamp, in the wax was left the impression of a peacock.

Percival Peacock held the envelope in his hands and stared at it for some time, rethinking what he was about to do. What he was about to entrust.

Percival glanced at the newspaper article beside him on the desk as he set down the envelope. His left hand touched the picture that filled one fourth of the newspaper page. It was of the Crypto-Capers Team. They were his only hope. Percival could take care of himself, being a powerful man with money and many connections, but through his years of experience with this particular predator close on his heels, he knew he was running out of time. The predator would be coming for him, and there would be no escape from their demands. He would have to comply. To strengthen his hand against the evil, he must run some interference, but would they do it? Would they accept the challenge to help him? Percival fervently hoped so.

Then Percival heard something different from the storm. A loud *CRASH!* It came from somewhere on the second floor. It almost sounded like a window had shattered. Percival knew this was impossible. The windows had indestructible glass. It was one of his recent safety measures. But wait . . . not all the windows had been refitted. A few on the second floor hadn't been changed over yet. The storm . . . a branch could have hit the glass. But he knew better even as he considered the possibility that the storm was to blame. No, this was not about the storm. The war had begun.

Percival Peacock stood up from his chair and grabbed the envelope and the newspaper article, shoving them both into his tan jacket pocket, which matched his tan trousers. Percival was a short man in his sixties. Not only was his hair as white as snow, but so was his mustache that curled at both ends. Wise and yet eccentric, he was known for his many oddities. He remained motionless, listening, for a long moment before a sound on the stairs spurred him into action. A slight breeze blew out the candle. Then, as if candles, the lights in the room also extinguished.

Gone was his relaxed composure. Panic began to consume him. His hands searched frantically for something in the main, middle drawer of his roll top desk. His fingers ran across a button. He pushed it. A secret compartment towards the back of the desk opened. Percival's breathing had quickened and he could feel sweat upon his brow as his hands moved with urgency into the compartment, toppling the candlestick and knocking over his pen set. He tried to take several deep breaths to calm himself, but was failing miserably. "Where is it?" he muttered to himself. He tried to see into the dark but could not. It was as if he were blind. Yes, that's it. He closed his eyes, allowing his memory to guide him. When his aging hands clenched the soft leather binding of his keepsake, he pulled it from the compartment and held it to his chest. Though his heart still pounded in his ears, his eyes had become accustomed to the gloom. He could make out little, but enough.

"They will not get it," vowed Percival as he glanced around his dark bedroom, a smile on his face as he thought of the many traps he had set for the ones coming after his prized possession. He had always known that one day it would come down to this moment. That was why he had spent many years preparing. Had the last few windows been changed to unbreakable glass, his mansion might have held the predator at bay. But now he had to deal with the situation.

Soon, Percival's composure was again calm as he moved swiftly to the wall on the other side of the room towards his closet, his arms out ahead of him so as not to trip on anything in his way or on the floor. He opened the door and slipped inside. Underneath the shelf in front of him he knew there was a button that blended seamlessly with the oak paneling. Percival's hand lightly passed over the wood, lighting on the button. He pressed it and a hidden door silently opened. He stepped inside, and the panel closed. He had vanished, leaving behind him more than just a mystery to solve.

ONE

DOWN AT SCOTLAND YARD, Max and Mia were talking to some of their detective friends, telling them about some of their adventures over the past month. Their friends, in turn, were sharing some of their stories and adventures. After briefly joining in the rendition, Granny easily slipped away to talk with Chief Inspector Jaffrey, her old friend, who had asked the team to come down to the Yard. Granny wanted to speak privately with him. Something had been bothering her since their last case, and she wished to have answers to her questions while she had the chance. Chief Inspector Jaffrey was sitting at his desk, finishing up a phone call when Granny half opened the door, stuck her head inside and knocked. She knew he was expecting her. He waved her in.

Chief Inspector Seamus Jaffrey was a freakishly large man. He appeared tall even when sitting. His bushy auburn handlebar mustache hung beneath his nose with panache. It really enhanced his appearance, and it had been years since Granny had seen him without it. His thick auburn hair was neatly trimmed and combed off to the side, and though his brilliantly ice-blue eyes often were serious, the wrinkles at the corners of his eyes revealed his sense of humor. He waved her to a chair as he continued on the phone. Granny entered the room, closing the door behind her, then headed towards a dark burgundy-red chair that appeared reasonably comfortable.

She held her large fuchsia handbag tightly to her side as she sat. The chair had not been a good choice. It was as uncomfortable to sit on as a cactus with springs poking her bony bottom with only a layer of fabric between. She shifted about, finding a position that at least didn't hurt. She raised her hand to her head and patted her grey-white bun, adjusting the chopsticks that held it in place.

Chief Inspector Jaffrey hung up the phone and placed his massive hands upon his desk. "I've heard about the cases you and your team have been taking on. Quite impressed, Nellie. Quite impressive indeed. I knew you could handle anything. You've been doing very well for yourselves, furthering your career and all that."

"Thank you, Chief Inspector. We've had many successes. Our decision to go on our own has been working out pretty well for us." Granny paused for a few seconds. "Congratulations on your promotion to chief inspector. You've been moving up in ranking pretty quickly. You must be pleased."

The Chief Inspector patted his desk with pride. "It has been a long time coming. I'm more than pleased."

Granny nodded in agreement. "You called us here for a reason, I know, but I must ask you something first while my grandchildren are occupied. You must promise to tell me the truth on the matter."

Chief Inspector Jaffrey leaned back in his chair, his right hand fingers curling around his mustache while his kind features hardened slightly. "I can make no promises, Nellie, you know that."

Granny narrowed her eyes at Chief Inspector Jaffrey, obviously displeased with his answer. "You know we've been after the notorious Panther."

"I do!"

"We've disclosed some of that information to you, so you could help us with the matter."

He lifted a beige file folder from his desk. "You have!"

"So, what I want to know is simply this. During our last encounter with the Panther, he said something, something that has been bothering me since then. He confided in Mia that my late husband, Harold, had been helping him with his evil endeavors." Granny paused, then in a softer voice, she said, "Could this be true?"

Chief Inspector Jaffrey didn't respond for several moments, then popped up from his chair as if on springs, his over six-foot frame moving towards the nearest window. With his back to Granny, he said, "He's dead, Nellie. You know that."

"So we thought!"

Chief Inspector Jaffrey turned his head toward Granny, a look of concern on his features.

Taking a breath, Granny said, "What I want to know is if it's possible that he could still be alive? No one could find his body. I remember Mitchem joining the recovery team and diving into those frigid waters searching for Harold's body after Scotland Yard said he had drowned. My son searched for days, fighting the currents, the cold, and the hopelessness. But in the end, after all the evidence was laid out, all the witnesses talked to, there was no concrete evidence that Harold had drowned."

"Nellie, the witnesses did confirm that two men, one having Harold's description, had fought violently near the water's edge. The men were yelling and hitting each other with bricks and boards found at the scene. Harold had been hit in the head with a heavy wooden crate. We know this. His blood was on the crate and was tested, confirmed to be his. The witnesses said he fell after being hit with that crate, and as he fell, he caught hold of his attacker's arm and dragged him over the edge of the wharf as he fell into the water."

"But neither body was found. If Harold could grab onto his attacker, he most surely was not dead. There was no evidence that Harold actually died, nor the other man."

"If Harold was hit in the head hard enough to lose consciousness, Nellie, there would have been no way for him to recover and swim away."

"But he grabbed onto the other man. Unconscious people don't grab."

Granny thought for a moment. Could the Panther have felt remorse or pity, actually helping Harold live? The possibility was certainly there, but seemed as unlikely a prospect. There were so many variables. Maybe it wasn't Harold who had been hit in the head, maybe it had been the reverse? But then his blood was on the crate proving his identity. Maybe the Panther hadn't been there at all. Maybe other men had been in shadows, in the water. Or was there more to it than that?

Chief Inspector Jaffrey could see the distracted expression on Granny's face. "Don't torture yourself, Nellie. Don't do this. Harold's dead and you must accept it. It's been five years."

Granny narrowed her eyes. "I do accept his death, and you know I've moved on." She waved her hands in the general direction of the other room, where her grandchildren still regaled an audience of detectives with their exploits. "I accept that deaths occur, that bodies go missing. I accept that because Harold has not returned in these five years. But, Seamus, the Yard would have access to the kind of information if it were true that indicated that Harold was . . . cooperating with the Panther. And if this were a covert operation orchestrated by the Yard—"

"Don't, Nellie! Don't go there!" Chief Inspector Jaffrey shouted, then lowered his voice, trying to control his emotions. "Are you seriously asking me if the Yard had anything to do with his disappearance? With his real or fake death? No, Nellie. Absolutely not. We had nothing to do with any of this. You know Harold was on assignment when he died, and yes, I sent him on that assignment. But we did not plan for what happened. I have no knowledge of Harold being alive, nor do I have any information that he was working for the enemy against us. It was a sad day for us all when he had passed, Nellie. He had a natural talent at solving cases, as does your whole family."

Chief Inspector Jaffrey's expression and voice softened. "I care for you, Nellie. We've known each other a long time. If it had been necessary for Harold to go underground, I wouldn't have allowed it without your knowing in advance that it was a possibility. I know what Harold meant to you. I wouldn't put you through that kind of pain." Chief Inspector Jaffrey could see Nellie's disappointment.

"But would your bosses?"

The Chief Inspector's forehead began to furrow. That was a good question. "If it'd ease your mind, I can dig a little deeper into the matter. Since I know nothing, if something like this does exist, it's above my pay grade. Could it be a possibility that Harold is still alive? Of course! As you say, we could not find his body. But here is the skinny of it, Nellie. I don't know if what the Panther said was the truth. Easily he could be trying to bamboozle you into thinking that Harold's alive—when in fact—he isn't. He could be tricking you, playing a game he feels he can win because he can win no other game against your team. He could be distracting you, trying to put you in a position of uncertainty. You know his games."

"Yes, I know. I've considered all this. But it doesn't mean that the Panther isn't telling us the truth. He seemed honest in his confession to Mia. I'm not sure what it is, but he often bares his soul to her and reveals more of his true identity than I believe he would otherwise. He revealed something that day. Something he wasn't supposed to reveal."

Chief Inspector Jaffrey walked over to Granny. She stood up from her chair to meet him. He placed his large hands on either side of her shoulders and squeezed. "I don't know why the Panther would confess things to Mia. Maybe he has a daughter somewhere, lost a daughter. Mia must remind him of her."

"I believe he said that, if he *had* a daughter, she would be like Mia," Granny interjected. "I don't think he would have said that, if in truth, he had a daughter."

Chief Inspector Jaffrey shook his head. "He would if he had wanted one, but was deprived of the opportunity."

Granny let out a long breath. There were so many possibilities, with so many possible answers.

"We know the Panther has a son. I don't know if he has other children. We're just speculating. Our background on him is limited. We only know about Denton, his son, because your team discovered that tidbit. If the Panther has other heirs—they're unknown to us at this time, which means they're probably well hidden if they exist. To be honest, our beef is not with them, unless they are involved directly with their father in some way. But I don't think anyone would mind speaking with them and learning more about the Panther's ways and history if we can discover them. Denton revealed very little about his father when questioned. It was almost as if he had been disconnected from him for years and didn't know a thing about him. Obviously, their bond has changed, according to your findings on your latest case."

Chief Inspector Jaffrey paused as Granny's head nodded. "If he had other children, we could lure him out of hiding with them. It would give us an advantage, which is why he obviously keeps them hidden. I bet a man who has a son could have more offspring." Chief Inspector Jaffrey's voice trailed off into a whisper. Then he thought of the possibilities.

Granny said, "If he has other children, Seamus, and they are not in contact with him, why bother them and exploit them? You'd be putting their innocent lives at risk for nothing but a possible bluff. You'd do that and ruin their lives? Their safety?"

Chief Inspector Jaffrey paused, then shook his head rapidly. "No! Well, maybe. Look, Nellie, business is business. It's not personal, so don't make it. It is what it is. If you say the Panther reveals information to Mia that you think might be significant, keep paying attention to it. It may help us catch him in the long run." Then he added, "Or not! He's a clever and elusive man. The Panther didn't become who he is because he tells the truth and is an honest man. His gambit is bringing doubt and drenching us with it. We have no fact here. Nothing we've said in this room is proven, just speculations and possibilities we might be hoping could be true. We know how far they go."

Not that far, thought Granny as she shook her head. Her features were stern, but after several seconds of thinking over the chief inspector's words, Granny's features softened. He had a point.

"I have more important news," the chief inspector said. "Mitchem and Martha are coming home from their last assignment. I received word just before you arrived." Then he added, resentfully, "Morris probably knows more about their exact location than I do. He's been tracking them for Max and Mia through our system, I'm sure. Tell him for me that he needs to stop doing that without authorization. Breaking into our system and accessing classified information is illegal. I noticed an anomaly in the system, but is unexplained. I'm going to write it off as a glitch in the system to my superiors because I have a gut feeling I know who put it there."

Granny tried to keep her features passive. "It's illegal to access your system without authorization, but it's legal when you ask Morris to hack into files to help you with certain matters of state? I believe you refer to it as a favor for a favor?" Granny knew what buttons to push. "Don't you think I know what my team does on their spare time?"

Chief Inspector Jaffrey cleared his throat.

"I don't think your superiors would appreciate that little tidbit, do you *Chief Inspector*?"

"Don't spew my rank out as if it were a bad taste in your mouth, Nellie. I know the deal we have. But not everything should go through that little wiz-kid. You know that."

"Oh, I know, but you also know that your duty is to protect him, especially if you want him to help you in the future."

Chief Inspector Jaffrey caught the slight threat. "Are you telling me he hasn't been trying to put some clarity to your concerns about Harold by digging into our files?"

"If he has, would I be here consulting you about the topic?" sassed Granny.

Chief Inspector Jaffrey leaned forward slightly. "You would if he couldn't find anything concerning Harold's resurrection."

Granny clenched her teeth. "Do you have proof that Morris has been accessing your system illegally, Seamus?"

Chief Inspector Jaffrey narrowed his eyes to slits, a smirk on his lips. "I have no proof that he does it without warrant, but I know full well he's capable and has access. Morris always seems to know more than we do concerning the Holmes' whereabouts. What else am I to think?"

"You forget, dear friend, that it's his job to know where we are at all times, and it's a job he does exceedingly well. I think you're a little paranoid about this."

Chief Inspector Jaffrey held up two fingertips with a tiny gap between them. "Maybe a smidge." Then he took a deep breath, exhaling sharply. "You're right, that's his job, and he's very discreet about it. He's one of the best hackers I know. Just tell him not to snoop around too much if he *is* accessing our system without authorization. To know more than one should might put him in danger, and believe me, it's not something I'm hiding. I care for your team, Nellie. I don't want them to get hurt, and right now there are some powerful people out there looking for a fight. Don't give them one."

9

Granny absorbed the advice. "The corruption of some people astounds me."

"Yes, well, it wouldn't take much for an enemy of yours, higher up on the chain of command, to apply the right pressure. You're safe for now. Your team's well received. Believe me, Scotland Yard feels your team is quite the asset. Let's keep it that way."

"I appreciate the advice, and it will be relayed," assured Granny as she drew several deep breaths.

"I have more advice to give. As a friend to a friend, I feel you need to take a holiday and spend some quality time with your family. You need it to clear your head, Nellie. I'll make sure your son doesn't leave again until you return from wherever you decide to lose yourself."

Granny glared at Chief Inspector Jaffrey in disbelief. "Running away from my concerns is not the answer I'm looking for, because, when I return, the concerns will still exist." Granny's anger was mixed with relief that her son would be coming home. She hadn't seen him in over a month. Granny took a deep breath and focused her attention in front of her. She wanted answers, yet knew she wasn't going to get any, so decided to change the topic entirely. "Why did you call us in here today?"

"I can have someone else take care of the problem. Don't worry about it." Chief Inspector Jaffrey let his hands drop from Granny's shoulders. He swiftly moved back around his desk to sit in his chair. His appearance resolute.

"You're such a liar," Granny said. "You'd have only called us in here if the job was something your men couldn't handle. Remember how long I've known you, Seamus. Now, tell me what you need."

Chief Inspector Jaffrey raised his hand to caress his mustache, a twinkle of knowing shining in his eyes. "Percival Peacock, the famous inventor, is missing. His mansion was broken into. We feel he has a connection with the Panther, and because no one has encountered the Panther more than your team, there's no one else better to help us figure out what happened. My men have surrounded the perimeter of the mansion, but no one has gone inside. To be honest, they aren't sure how. The place is . . . amazingly booby trapped. And there's some kind of barrier or something like that. I don't know, but we have a real problem. I need the skill of your team to help us find Percival Peacock. He's the only one who can tell us the Panthers true identity."

"What makes you think he will divulge it?"

"Let's just say that he has something valuable that will interest us all. With the corner he's been forced into, he's like a mouse in front of a hungry cat, with nowhere to run. He has no choice but to divulge it, and he will do so to save himself. I'm counting on it." Granny narrowed her eyes.

"Scotland Yard wasn't the cat, was it?"

Chief Inspector Jaffrey scoffed, shaking his head at the implication that Scotland Yard would have instigated the assault upon Percival. "No, not at all! Not us. We have nothing on him to be that ferocious cat, but I would be lying if I said that I wasn't thrilled to find him in that corner. He's an amazing man. I'm eager to learn what he knows."

"What does he know?"

"A tremendous amount, I'm afraid. He knows who's responsible for the corruption of this fair city. There are lots of honest men who want what's best for England, but their voices are being drowned out by the corrupted and evil doers. I have no proof to change anything, to create an upset so big that it would turn our economy around. Percival has that information—and more. He knows facts about people. He has a connection with the Panther. There's a history there we need to understand. In so doing, we will find the Panther's weakness. If we know more about him, we can take him down."

"I wouldn't count on Percival giving up too much information, Seamus. He's elusive for a reason. He's definitely not an imbecile either. Yet, I can see his dilemma. We'll work with Scotland Yard and provide you with whatever information Percival Peacock gives to us. I hope it's what you expect it to be." Chief Inspector Jaffrey smiled confidently.

"It will be. The one thing I know is that your team can impress anyone." Chief Inspector Jaffrey lifted a folder from his desk. "Here's the folder on Percival. Read it over with your team and let me know how I can assist." Granny reached for the thick folder. "Keep me informed of all actions. We will be working together, joining forces on this case. I'll be notifying you of our liaison once the officer has been identified."

"Make sure you send us someone competent. I don't feel like training another one." Granny's comment produced a smirk out of Chief Inspector Jaffrey.

"Don't fret. The person I'll assign to your team will have the experience you need to assist you." Chief Inspector Jaffrey revealed a sly smile, his eyes narrowing.

Granny narrowed her eyes in return. She'd heard the tone in his voice and the hint of mischievousness. Granny held up her pointer finger, her mouth open to question, but Chief Inspector

Jaffrey beat her to it, his tone now serious. "Yes, I'll also look more into what we talked about concerning Harold. It's the least I can do for you. But please heed my advice, Nellie. I give it with care."

"I know you do." Granny paused slightly, debating on changing the topic. As she pondered what to say and how to say it, she felt as if she were walking on thin ice on a spring pond. "Tell Corinth I miss her. We should get together sometime soon."

Chief Inspector Jaffrey's features softened slightly, his lips curling into a smile. "My wife would love that. It has been awhile since you've spent time with her. She misses you, too. Some of her fondest memories are with you. She says you could always make her laugh."

Corinth Jaffrey and Granny had been friends for years. They had met their husbands about the same time and had often comforted each other when their husbands were away. Their friendship had changed though, since Harold had died. They had spent less time together and when they did, Granny couldn't help but feel out of place. Granny knew she should rekindle the bond between them, but she found it extremely hard to jumpstart it. It felt like torture, but, boy, would it feel good to have someone else to bare her feelings too. Corinth would understand. She always did.

"M—Maybe we could get together for tea? That would be nice, wouldn't it?"

Chief Inspector Jaffrey laughed softly, nodding his head. "She would like that very much. I'll have her call you."

"Thank you!"

Chief Inspector Jaffrey saw Granny's misted expression, and he was about to say more, but his phone rang. Gone was the friend and the smile, replaced by the stern business-minded Chief Inspector Jaffrey.

"Good luck with the case, Nellie. Good day!" The curtness in Chief Inspector Jaffrey's tone made it quite clear to Granny that the conversation was finished. She picked up her handbag, smiled sweetly and walked out of the room to where Max and Mia were waiting for her in the hallway, the folder held tightly in her grip.

TWO

OUTSIDE THE AIR WAS TURNING BITTERLY COLD. A storm had drenched them coming in, but now the rains had stopped, replaced by winds that howled menacingly. Puddles lay all over the sidewalks and streets with larger areas that were partially flooded, causing a hazard to the cars driving in the city of London. The people on the sidewalks had to be careful to avoid street puddles the cars hit or find themselves bathed in dirty water and soaked beyond immediate recovery. Winter was on its way, yet with these storms, fall refused to surrender its hold on the country. The team had recently traveled to the Riviera Maya, Portugal, and Italy. They had been quite spoiled by warm, decent weather. They were immersed now in the more unpredictable temperament of London's weather.

Cold was settling in, and the damp chill sank into their bones, especially when the icy wind whipped without mercy. Granny had been quiet as they rode the London Underground Railway, not saying a word about her conversation with Chief Inspector Jaffrey. Even when they had reached the Baker Street Tube Station, she still held her silence, walking with a purpose until they stepped out of the station and onto the junction of Marylebone Road and Baker Street.

The Baker Street Tube Station was only a short distance from their apartment. They used the London Underground quite often to get from one place to another. It beat having to deal with London's weather. When they emerged, the wind whipped them with renewed vengeance as they hurried to the building entrance. The lobby was empty as they walked inside. Max checked their mailbox, which had only a few envelopes in it, before following Granny and Mia to a locked staircase off to the right, and they made the short jaunt up the few floors of stairs to their flat.

Max and Mia could tell that something was bothering Granny, and they knew precisely what it was without even asking, which was why they weren't pushing her to converse. She was wondering if their grandfather could be alive after all these years. Max had remembered the evidence of the case, but there was no definitive proof that their grandfather had not drowned. All evidence pointed to the contrary. They were all letting their minds run away with them as far as Max was concerned, letting the crafty Panther mess with their heads.

Mia, on the other hand, could still feel the warmth of the Panther's breath by her cheek when he had divulged the information to her. The smug look on his features as he had said it made Mia feel sick to her stomach. She didn't want to believe it if it was true, but Max had another mind about the matter completely.

He wanted to leave nothing to chance. Their grandfather being alive was a possibility, and it left room for doubt in his mind, which was probably exactly what the Panther wanted to do. If their grandfather was a traitor, it was going to be a hard pill to swallow, but Max and Mia knew many things about solving a mystery and being detectives. One of the most important was never to assume you know the answer until you have collected and studied all of the facts. But all the facts were not available about their grandfather, nor, if he was alive, his side of the story. Only after hearing that and considering what that meant could they decide where truth lay. That left them in a kind of limbo, with no way to make a decision and only assumptions and hard feelings left to them.

"What did Chief Inspector Jaffrey say?" asked Max as they walked into their apartment, finally pushing the matter. The warmth of the apartment filled them as they unzipped their coats. Granny took off her jacket and placed it on the coat rack by the door. She then dropped her handbag on the floor and walked into the kitchen to get a drink. She tossed the file folder onto the counter top.

"Go ahead and look for yourself," Granny replied tersely. Max and Mia hung up their coats as well. Mia glanced at Max before walking over to the counter top and opening the file folder. Max placed the mail on the counter beside it. Before anything could be read, Morris walked out from the secret room he had been working on for some time. It was now completely finished, with a brand new top-notch alarm system that he had installed especially for it.

"Hey, I have some news for you," spouted Morris excitedly as he closed the door to the room by pressing his hand against the wall. Inside of the wall was a secret sensor that recognized the contours of Morris's hand. The door snapped closed as Morris's tall lanky form filled the doorway. His hair was slicked back away from his face and he was wearing a pair of jeans with a button-down blue shirt. He looked much neater than the dingy stained t-shirts he usually wore.

"What's the occasion?" asked Mia, glancing at him.

"I'm trying something new. What do you think?"

Mia gave Morris a crooked smile as her eyes traveled up and down Morris's slim physique. She knew better. "I like it. So, when is Liliana calling?"

Morris's eyes grew wide. Then, realizing he wasn't fooling anyone, glanced at the clock on the wall. "Her webcam should be up in about twenty minutes."

"Uh, huh," replied Mia as she shook her head.

"What's the news?" asked Max.

"Oh, your parents are on their way back from their latest mission. According to their GPS, they are at the first check point in Moscow. Two more to go before they'll be secure enough to return to England."

Excitement filled Mia and Max's features. "When do you think they will arrive?" asked Mia excitedly.

"In about four or five days, I'd say. They'll have to brief Scotland Yard upon their return and then they'll arrive here shortly after that."

"Good! That'll give us time to solve another mystery," Granny said coming out of the kitchen with a cup of hot tea in her hands. She plopped onto the sofa, using one hand to tweak the chopsticks in her hair.

"Is that what Chief Inspector Jaffrey wanted to talk to us about?" asked Morris. "A new case?"

Granny nodded as she slurped her tea, closing her eyes to enjoy the relaxing honey and chamomile flavor and warmth.

"He wants us to help locate someone."

"Who?" said Max, Mia, and Morris in unison.

Granny pointed a finger towards the countertop where the folder was opened. All three heads seemed to turn at once. They caught their first glimpse of Percival Peacock's picture.

"Our missing person is Percival Peacock?" spouted Morris in disbelief. "He's one of the most imaginative and charismatic inventors I've ever run across, and one of the most successful. He's created inventions for many important people, including our military."

"Yes, but he's also created some oddball inventions that people have made fun of him for," added Mia as she perused the papers in the folder, brushing her blond hair away from her face. "As of late it seems he's considered more of an after dinner joke. He's eccentric to the point, almost, of being an outcast."

"That's because no one ever believed in him," concluded Morris. "The man's a genius."

"He's a man who has patents for some of the most unusual things. It says here that he has patented over one hundred ideas. Some of them useful, but some outrageously inappropriate," added Max.

"What exactly happened to him?" interrupted Morris as he glanced eagerly over at Granny.

"Chief Inspector Jaffrey seems to think that Percival disappeared because someone was after him. He has something—"

"The Peacock Diaries!" inserted Morris quickly, as he stared off into space for a moment.

Granny, Max and Mia all stared at Morris.

"The what?" asked Max.

"The Peacock Diaries! Percival Peacock keeps a series of diaries that encompasses years of his inventions, from his not so popular ideas and creations, to the ones that made him rich, and everything in between. He has names, addresses, account numbers, you name it, of all his clients and would-be clients he's researched."

Granny's eyes opened wide, as she remembered something.

"That was what Chief Inspector Jaffrey meant. He said that Percival knows the true identity of the Panther."

A crooked grin formed on Max's lips. "Then by all means, we must indeed help solve this mystery. What do we know about what happened?"

"Not much. The report says that Percival lives in the Lake District in the county of Cumbria, in Keswick on Derwent Island. He owns quite a bit of property in that district. The Derwent Island House is an historic eighteenth-century house, standing on a small wooded isle in the center of the lake. The house stands within a restored period garden. The picture here is amazing."

Max leaned over the photo. "The island's very remote. Anything could happen out there, and no one know anything about it. Who put the call into the police?"

"It says here that it was a woman, an Edith Simpleton. She lives in Keswick and brings groceries to the house once a week every Monday at noon. She came to the house to make her delivery when she noticed the broken window. Her agreement with Percival was that she would leave the groceries in a basket near the front of the house. She's never been inside nor has she ever seen Percival. He leaves money for her in a secret spot (she wouldn't say where). He calls her from the house the day before to let her know what he needs from the store. The food is paid for in advance."

"Is there anyone else with access to the island?" asked Granny.

"The only other people who come to the island are landscapers hired to maintain the grounds. No one at the company has ever seen Percival either. There's a confidentiality agreement between him and the landscapers. He pays them well so they'll disclose nothing. They've never been inside of the house either," replied Mia.

"What did the police say in the report?" asked Morris.

"They said that access to the house is . . . difficult. Despite the many windows, the majority of the glass is shatterproof. They're also locked and impossible to open from the outside. There's no obvious front or back doors, and the police said they were not able to get inside. They did see one window smashed with a rock on the second floor. Their speculation is that the intruders brought a ladder and were able to get in through that window, but . . ."

"But what?"

"Well, it says they weren't able to get out of the room. The report says they were chased and attacked by . . . regular household objects."

"What does that mean? Did someone . . . throw stuff at the police? Or were objects rigged to attack intruders?" inquired Granny.

"I think they were definitely made to attack intruders. The police said they just appeared in the shapes of snakes and birds. For example, one man noted that a normal book changed before his eyes into a large king cobra that attacked him, biting his arm. Fortunately there was no venom. Needless to say the men bolted from the room so fast that one man was injured falling off the ladder."

"If there were disguised snakes and birds in that room, what do the other rooms contain?" inquired Max.

No one volunteered anything because, quite frankly, no one knew.

"This is going to be a difficult case indeed." Having gone through the file, Max ruffled through the pile of mail he had tossed onto the counter top. The Crypto-Capers team received notes from fans, thank-yous from clients, and, often, queries for help. None of the mail seemed particularly interesting until Max came to a beige envelope. What stood out was the wax seal on the back. He ran a finger over the wax. Stamped in it was an impression of a peacock.

"Ah, gang . . ." Max began.

THREE

"LOOK AT THIS!" SAID MAX AS HE HELD up the envelope. When the rest seemed non-plussed, he pointed out the seal. That drew everyone to the counter.

"You don't think . . ." began Granny.

"It's from him," interjected Morris. "But why? Why would he contact us? We aren't of any use to him."

"On the contrary, Morris," said Mia, "we could be of great use to him. He wants us to save him and if not him, then maybe the diaries. What we do and how we solve cases is not a mystery. As of late, the newspaper has been taking liberties with our photos, splashing them all over the front page and such."

Mia walked over to a desk in the corner and rifled through a stack of newspapers piled there. When she found the one she was looking for, she pulled the page out and folded it in half. "Like this one. This is a picture of us taken by a journalist after our last case. This isn't the first picture taken of us, either. Now, look at the title, it says, 'England's Youngest and Bravest Detectives Almost Capture the Notorious Panther!' they might as well staple targets to our chests, and that's what notice like this is going to become if they continue extolling our exploits. But that being said, I believe Percival could easily have seen this article and he might believe that we could help him in some way. We're the only ones who've really been able to get close and personal with the Panther. If the Panther is after Percival or his diaries for reasons unknown to us, maybe we could stop him."

"The papers want us to become their hottest story, Mia," said Max. "Unfortunately, they'll never go away. But I think you might be right about Percival." Max broke the seal, opened the envelope and pulled out the letter. As he lifted the folds he saw a brief message, a very brief message. Written in the prettiest calligraphy he had ever seen were the following words.

"Looking for answers? Go to the Globe!"

"The Globe? What's he talking about?" asked Mia as she read the words over Max's shoulders.

"I don't know. If he's talking about the planet, that's not much of a clue. What else could it be?" Max was confused as he read the words again.

"Globe is capitalized, Max," Morris pointed out as he glanced over the other shoulder. "It must be a place."

"The Globe Theatre then?" The answer came from Granny, still slurping her tea. "It's here in Bankside, near Southwark London. It's not that far away. Percival must have hidden something there for us."

Max grinned. "Anybody up for a quick jaunt?"

"I'm shattered," said Granny, taking up her place on the couch again and curling up her legs. "My bones ache from the cold. I'll stay here. But the rest of you can go. I doubt all of our skills will be needed for this. The plays usually run all year round but I recently read in the paper that the theater is currently closed for repairs and won't open again for a few weeks. They're only allowing touring schools and organizations inside."

"I'll pass on the field trip as well, but you and Mia can go, Max," said Morris. "Liliana will be coming up soon on the webcam. I don't want to miss her. She's done some research for me I'm looking forward to getting. I'll be able to hear you through the new ear pieces. Wear them. Try them out. I can still talk with you through the watch phones if needed, but let's see what the ear pieces can do."

Max glanced at Mia. "I guess it's just you and me then. Grab your backpack and we'll be off."

Mia nodded as she hurried to her room for her backpack. On the way she considered what else she might want to take with them. "Are you sure neither of you wants to come?" Max asked one more time.

"Sure!" Granny replied firmly. "Besides, Morris and I need to talk."

Morris glanced at Granny. He had a feeling he knew what she was going to discuss. "You mean you want to talk about accessing Scotland Yard's computer systems?"

"You did what?" interjected Max, surprised. "Who asked you to do that?"

"Morris!" Granny warned.

He ignored her and answered Max's question. "Granny did. I accessed it upon her request." Morris then turned to Granny who was looking annoyed. "And, no, I won't keep quiet about it. You shouldn't be keeping secrets from them anyway." Morris chided.

Granny raised her hand, stopping Morris's rant. "I know what I asked you to do, which is why I defended you in front of Chief Inspector Jaffrey when he mentioned noticing a breach into his system. He knows there is an anomaly."

"No, there's not!" Morris shot back. "No way. I can slip into that system and back out without any alerts."

"What did you ask Morris to dig up for you, Granny?" Max asked Granny quietly.

Her cheeks flushed. "Nothing important, I was just curious about something."

"Granddad perhaps?" Max's calculated words caused Granny's cheeks to flush more deeply.

"I don't want to talk about it, Max."

"But, Granny, we need to talk about it. We need to get it out in the . . ."

"Not right now we don't, Maxwell. I'm not ready to open up about it yet."

"But you're ready to get Morris nicked by the police? Hacking Scotland Yard is a serious crime. And it risks our relationship with Scotland Yard for digging into their files. You know we have to be careful when hacking into a government system. There are consequences—serious ones—if we're caught."

Granny shook her head. "It's not like that. I'm just trying to figure out what's truth and what's a lie. That's all. I know what I'm doing."

"You probed Chief Inspector Jaffrey about Grandad didn't you? What did he say?"

Granny shook her head, not wanting to answer. But Max already knew. "He knows nothing, doesn't he? Which means that your doubts are unfounded, Granny. Granddad is dead. Let's face this fact and move on. I can't believe you were hiding this from me—from us." Max looked disappointed as he raised his arms in frustration. Morris didn't look any happier. Both boys knew there was more to be said, but Granny didn't look like she was going to say any more about it.

"All I'm saying to you, Morris, is to be more cautious when digging into the updated system of Scotland Yard. Chief Inspector Jaffrey knows someone accessed the files and he was pretty sure it was you, but he told his people it was just a glitch in the system."

"Well, it's not surprising he'd guess it was me. Problem is, it might not be me. He knows what I can do, because of all the favors I've done for him. He should protect me."

"That's exactly what I mentioned to him," replied Granny. "But he wanted to make sure he mentioned the recent changes they've made to the system. He did so to prevent hackers from accessing it, yet he also gave you a heads up about it. Don't worry, I had your back."

"Good, because you're the one with the crazy requests," said a frustrated Morris.

"I'm going to forget you said that," spouted Granny as she sipped her tea.

Morris sighed. "It's forgotten!"

"All righty, then," interrupted Mia as she came back into the room. She'd heard enough of the conversation to account for three angry, frustrated faces.

Max took a deep breath. "Morris, we'll apprise you of what we find at the theatre. Granny, we'll keep in touch."

"All right dears, just be careful." Granny's tone was back to casual, with no hint of tension. Max and Mia nodded as they walked out the front door, heading towards the secret elevator.

Once on the main floor and out the door, they immediately hopped on a bus that took them to the Bankside entrance of the Globe Theatre. Before they got off they checked the bus schedule. They waited for the bus to drive off before moving towards the theatre. The outside of the building was unique in design and appeared to have multiple sides like an octagon. The outer building was white with brown accents. It contained several small windows on its sides on the various levels,

three it appeared, though it was hard to tell. They saw few doors but no direct entrance into the building.

"Morris, we're at the theatre. What can you tell us about it?" The new ear pieces made their conversation more private. They no longer had to lift their wrists to their mouths, and Morris's side of the conversation was completely inaudible to passersby. This new equipment was high-tech even for earpieces, experimental actually, something they were able to get their hands on through one of Morris's contacts. The ear piece was small with the slightest hint of color, virtually undetectable once inserted in the ear. Max and Mia had put them in on the bus and were both wearing them. They could hear Morris's voice crystal clear and barely had to whisper for him to hear them. And, Max could also hear Mia even if he couldn't hear her speaking aloud.

"I'm here, team. My research tells me that the present Globe Theatre you're looking at was officially named 'Shakespeare's Globe' and was opened in 1997. It was built approximately 230 meters away from the original theatre used in Shakespeare's time. The original Globe Theatre was built in 1599 by Shakespeare's playing company known as the Lord Chamberlain's Men, which was later changed to the King's Men. That theatre was destroyed in a fire set off by cannon fire used during a play. The original partially thatched roof caught on fire. The theatre was rebuilt in about six months, using some timbers from the old theater. This time they added a partially tiled roof. The theatre was then closed in 1642 and torn down in 1644 by the Puritans, and housing was built on the site.

"The Globe was built in a similar style to the Coliseum in Ancient Rome, but on a much smaller scale. You could probably guess that by the roundness of it. Elizabethan theatres followed this style of architecture, called amphitheatres. When you look inside there really isn't a bad seat in the house. Unfortunately, not all buildings used in the theatre are built this way, at least not the ones I've seen, but they should be."

"That was a wealth of information, Morris. I do love the theatre," said Mia as she glanced at her brother.

Reddish-brown brick lined the walls near the street and swept up a set of wide stairs to an entrance blocked by a wrought iron gate. The gate stood at least fifteen to twenty feet tall and was decorated with eye-catching motifs. Nothing like it in the world could duplicate the eclectic wonder of the gate. Mia and Max placed their hands on the gate and touched the motifs. After touching several, Mia's eyes glistened with understanding.

"Max, these motifs were inspired by lines in Shakespeare's works. Look at this one, it's a mermaid. I remember it from reading *King Henry VI*, part 3. Richard speaks of it. He says, 'That he will drown more sailors than the Mermaid shall.' This is so bloody brilliant. Who came up with this idea?"

"An architect named Theo Crosby came up with the idea, Mia," Morris said. "He passed away before it could come to fruition, though. But his choice of friends was stellar. He worked with Richard Quinnell, who made sure that Theo's idea came to light. I'll see if I can pull up a key to the location of all the motifs. It might come in handy in future." Morris went to work.

Mia and Max began to count the motifs on the gate. All together there were sixty-three.

"Ohhh, this is brilliant," exclaimed Morris. "I pulled up a key to the Bankside Gates. There are a total of one hundred and twenty-five motifs on the gates."

"Not on this gate," replied Max. "There's only sixty-three here."

"Is there another gate?" asked Mia.

"Yes. On the backside of the building facing the Thames. It has the rest. That gate goes from sixty-four to one hundred and twenty-five motifs, so the other half. Take pictures of both gates before you leave, will you? In fact, take several. I'll analyze them as they come through." Mia pulled her camera out from her backpack and began to take several pictures. With the height of the gates Mia had to step on Max's shoulders to get close enough to take a picture of the top. She also had a clear view of the other side of the wall where a few flag poles stood.

"What are you doing?" asked a soft inquisitive voice from the other side of the gate. Mia slid down from Max's shoulders and put away her camera, pulling out her badge instead, as did Max.

"Excuse us, ma'am. We're just admiring the beauty of these gates. My name is Max Holmes, and this is my sister, Mia. We're detectives and are . . ." Max wasn't able to finish his sentence, the look on the woman's elderly features forced him to stop. The woman appeared thin under her thick jacket. Her modern glasses slid to the middle of her nose where her steel-blue eyes could scan with preciseness. She looked surprised, yet she quickly composed herself.

"You're Maxwell Sherlock Holmes? The leader of the Crypto-Capers detective team?"

"Yes!"

The woman looked quickly to her left, then to her right. She instantly stepped forward, pulling out a key as she did so and opened the gate.

"Quickly! I know what you're here for. Follow me!" The woman's tone was urgent.

Max and Mia wasted no time moving through the gate. The woman closed and locked it behind them. "This way!"

The woman set a fast pace, and it was hard to keep up, but they followed her to a set of doors where the entrance to the theatre was located. The door was locked, but the woman had a key out and ready. When the door was open, Max and Mia walked through. The woman closed the door behind them, but didn't lock it. She led the way into the theatre. The sight before them was impressive.

The stage was towards the back of the building with tall pillars on either side that appeared to be made of brown marble, set on a green base. There was a large area in front of the stage where people could stand and watch the performance. As they moved to the center of that area, Mia spun quickly on her heels. They were almost surrounded by the three galleries where people could sit on hard wood bench seats. It was amazing. This new Globe was built with a similar design to the old Globe built by Shakespeare. It was eerily familiar and yet impressive and inspiring.

"Look to the left of the stage," said the woman. "You'll find what you seek there. Take it and go. Here's the key. Leave it in the hole. I'll retrieve it later."

The woman handed Max a key with a round end. As Max and Mia stepped forward, Max turned to ask the woman a question, but was greeted with the sound of a closing door. The woman had disappeared leaving them alone.

"All right, Mia, impress me with your knowledge about the theater. What are some of the areas called?" Mia couldn't quite get over what she was experiencing.

"Well," Mia began, spreading her arms, "before us is the main stage. We're standing in the area known as the pit. To the back of the stage are doors leading to an area where actors could change or props were kept. The area above the main stage that's enclosed is known as the upper stage. Surrounding us is known as the gallery. This is a three-tiered area where people can watch. The stage is the center of attraction so it's an amphitheater. It's pretty basic."

They approached the left side of the stage.

Set into the side of the stage was a large plaque. As Max stepped forward, he read the words "*Totus mundus agit histrionem.*" Not knowing what the words meant, Max glanced at Mia, who shrugged.

"Granny?" spoke Max.

"Yes, dear?"

"*Totus mundus agit histrionem.*"

Granny was quiet for several seconds as her mind wrapped around the words. "The whole world is a playhouse. Anything else?"

"No, we're set. Thanks!" Max glanced at Mia as his fingers pressed upon his chin.

"That is the motto of the Globe Theatre," revealed Mia. "Shakespeare reworded this phrase in his play *As You Like It*. He wrote that, 'All the world's a stage,' but added, 'And all the men and women merely players.' Look at the stage. There's an overhang above it known as the 'Heavens,' in the day and was painted with a blue sky and clouds. That was where certain equipment was stored. The trap door in the floor of the stage was known as 'Hell.' That area was used for storage and where some of the entrances for the bad characters arose from. The stage represented life and the struggles between both places. The closer one stood to the trapdoor the closer to Hell they were, representing a character that was evil. Further away, the characters were trying to be closer to the Heavens, and in turn were probably good characters."

Mia's words were deep. Max never thought the world of theatre could have had so much meaning.

Near the bottom edge of the plaque was a keyhole. Max said, "I thought she was giving me the key to the gate, but . . ." and he placed the key into the hole. It fit. He turned it and heard a soft "click." He then lifted the plaque. Tucked inside of a wooden space was an envelope. Max reached for it. He closed the plaque and relocked it, leaving the key in its keyhole as the woman had ordered. On the front of the envelope, written in the same beautiful script as the letter that had come to their house, was his name. On the back was the seal of a peacock in wax, just like the first letter. Max glanced at his sister before opening the envelope. He proceeded to pull out the paper and unfold it. Then he began to read it quietly aloud.

Dear Crypto-Caper Team,

My name is Percival Peacock. You may have heard of me, or maybe not, but I am reaching out to you for help. I am an inventor of sorts. The one thing about inventing something is that you bare your soul with each new invention. Over the years my creativity has brought me good fortune, and bad. I believe we have a familiar enemy. His name is the Panther. By the time you read this, I will be gone. Hidden away where the Panther cannot reach out to strike, but I leave behind many things of importance. I feel we can help each other. We both want the Panther to be caught. The only way we can accomplish this goal is to work together.

Over the years the Panther has had many identities. But his career started here, in England, in the theater. A very talented man the Panther is, but a more brilliant student. He has learned much since his school days. I beseech you to come to my house and search the mysteries within. Only you four will be able to crack the code. Each room holds a puzzle that needs to be solved. Do this and your reward will be great. I will reveal to you the Peacock Diaries, only the one concerning our common friend, of course. Do you accept the challenge, or will it go unanswered? I do not figure your team for fools, but, if you don't accept the challenge, you will never find out the truth about the Panther's identity or who and what he is after next and why. I assure you it will be worth your while.

I implore you, take great care. My challenges are not for the faint of heart. You must be prepared to enter into my home. Be cautious. Do not be so foolish to believe you will be the only one in search of the diaries. Do not trust anyone you meet along the way. Believe in the members of your team. Unfortunately, the world of man is corrupt and full of greed. Man's alliances can be bought. I look forward to meeting you.

Good Luck!

Percival Percillius Peacock"

The letter consisted of two pages, with writing only on one side of each. Max turned the pages over, but he saw nothing out of the ordinary, so he returned the pages to the envelope.

"What now?" asked Mia.

"Percival sent us here in search of this letter, but there is more truth here to find, I'm sure of it. The gates were a clue. We can't ignore that. Percival hid this letter from someone. Otherwise he would have just put it in the post like the other. Someone intercepting the other letter wouldn't know what we have discovered and would miss so much. Percival was wise to do this, though he was taking a risk, hoping that one of the Panther's accomplices didn't follow his paper trail ahead of us," stated Max. "Let's leave out the back door facing the Thames and take pictures of that gate. We might need that information for future use."

Max tucked the letter into his pocket and led the way to the back entrance of the theatre.

FOUR

AN HOUR LATER, MAX AND MIA WALKED through their front door. After they hung up their coats, which were crisp from the cold air, Max removed the envelope from his pocket, took out the pages and spread them onto the table for Morris and Granny to read. These two new pages lay alongside the letter they had originally received through the post directly from Percival. In return, Morris, showed them the map key to the gates.

"Did you receive the pictures I took?" asked Mia as she glanced at the key of motifs.

"Yes, I have them right here on my computer. They're truly amazing."

"See what you two missed?" teased Max. "That's what you get when you stay behind. You miss out on many revelations."

"Yes, well, but we are now rested and ready to get things going," said Granny. "Morris was able to collect some information from Liliana while helping you, and I was able to calm myself and ease my mind." She made a graceful yoga move.

Max smiled at Granny. He laughed to himself as he thought of her practicing yoga in the middle of the room. He laughed louder when he saw her blue floor mat half stuffed underneath the couch.

"Where is the Panther now, Morris?"

Morris gave him a half smile. He knew Max was going to ask the question so was prepared for it. "The Panther is still where we left him. He's in Sydney, Australia. He hasn't moved from that location," revealed Morris. "I'm positive he's after Percival Peacock for the information he has that will lead us to his true identity. But I'm not sure if he knew that Percival would contact us directly. That would be out of character for Percival, who's been a pretty solitary man. Remember, the Panther, at times, doesn't think everything through. He's bloody brilliant and a master at deception nonetheless. The fact that he has never been caught, says that he's not a fool."

"But he has access to many accomplices, fools who would gladly do his bidding for him," added Mia.

Granny added, "Let's not forget that he now has Denton doing his dirty work for him as well, his own son. My concern is that Denton will follow down his father's path and once there, won't like what he finds. When that happens, I fear he still won't be able to change his ways. I don't think he realizes how dangerous his father really is. Denton doesn't have the skills or talents his father possesses. Which will lead to his capture more readily," observed Granny. "I bet it was Denton who initiated the attack against Percival. Maybe the threat was enough to put him into hiding. Maybe that was what he wanted, knowing that Percival's house could not be penetrated."

"It sounds logical, but as we know, logic doesn't always come into play," analyzed Mia. "I doubt it will in this situation and certainly not with these players, though your reasoning is sound. But, you show compassion for Denton, Granny—you shouldn't. We can't turn him. He's still a boy eager to please his father. Let's not forget that. He'll do whatever his father asks him to do. And Denton also has skills. He's clever and resourceful. He'll be the one to rally the accomplices, enact the tasks his father sets forth. Denton is a fool, there's no doubt, but we can't underestimate his abilities. He's determined, and once the Panther reveals to him his secrets in escaping the world, there'll be no stopping him either. He'll accomplish more than what any of us will expect, including his father. You can count on that."

Mia's words brought silence to the room. It also caused Max's forehead to furrow in concern.

"What are we to do?" asked Morris.

"Play the game Percival Peacock set forth," Max said. "He desperately wants us to win against the Panther, but he can't give us the answers for fear that the information will be intercepted by the Panther or his men. We have to earn them, which is why he set up this journey for us to take. We began at the Globe, but will now proceed to Percival's house and go through and solve his puzzles and whatever else he's laid out for us. He warned us to be ready, so we must be. Morris, show us all the new gadgets you've been working on and what they can do. We'll pack everything strategically and set out for Percival's house in the country in a few hours. It'll take us four or five hours to get to the Derwent House anyway, so that'll give us each a chance to rest, though Granny will have to drive." Max arched his eyebrows and shook his head at the thought.

"Or we can just take the train. That would probably be the best course. The safest course," Mia added before turning her head away from Granny, remembering how she drove the golf cart on their case in Florida. That was the only time she had driven anything, at least as far as any of them had ever seen, though Granny always insisted that she had driven a car before.

"Or we could just walk." Mia's whispered words caused Max's lips to curve into a smile. He had to hold back a chuckle by clearing his throat.

"No, I'll drive," blurted Granny. "I assure you I'm up to the task."

"Okay, but is their an auto?" Mia asked.

Morris and Max laughed out loud then, not being able to help themselves. But Granny didn't seem to share their sense of humor. She squared her narrow shoulders and lifted her chin. "I'll drive!" He voice and features were resolute.

The team had to give in, and their smiles and features turned serious once more. Silence hung in the air like smog for a matter of a few awkward seconds before they all heard the chimes of the door bell. Granny glared one more time at the group before striding to the door and glancing through the peep hole.

Granny seemed surprised, but she opened the door slowly, revealing Reginald, the man she was dating. His arrival was unexpected.

Guests of the apartment building had an option to use the elevator or stairs towards the back of the building. That was there only entrance and those locations were heavily supervised. Tenants could also use the coded, secured staircase to get to their apartments or the unobtrusively hidden elevator, which also lowered to a level underneath the building that led to a set of underground stairs leading away from the building. The security of the place was a bit extreme for what appeared to be an average

41

apartment building on a street filled with apartment buildings, but it had to be secure because the only tenants of this particular building were families of government agents, some hiding under false names.

"Hello, Reggie. What are you doing here?"

Reginald was a handsome man with salt-and-pepper black hair. He was the same age as Granny, in his sixties. He took extremely good care of his appearance, which showed in his muscular arms and legs. His skin, tan from his travels, made his eyes shine like sapphires, and they could melt even the coldest of hearts.

"I haven't heard from you in a week, Nellie. You haven't returned my calls or answered your phone. I was getting worried."

Before Granny could say a word, Reggie swept her up in his arms and kissed her. Granny tried to resist but soon melted like chocolate in the microwave. When the kiss ended, Granny stood straight and fixed her hair that had come undone. She looked at her grandchildren and Morris with embarrassment.

"Come in, Reggie," offered Granny as she backed into the room.

Feeling awkward, each team member made some excuse as to why they had to leave the room.

"I need to pack," blurted Mia.

"Didn't you want to show me something?" asked Max to Morris whose eyes were wide and bulging.

"Uh . . . yeah . . . it's over here in the other room." Morris, Max and Mia all left the room as quickly as they could, stumbling a bit.

Reggie unbuttoned his dark navy coat and hung it up on a peg on the wall. He then ran a hand through his short hair.

"I don't understand what's going on, Nellie. I know we have somewhat of a long-distance relationship at times. But, I thought we were going along great. Weren't we?" Reggie flopped his hands to his sides as he faced Nellie, his tone soft and curious.

"We were . . . *are* doing great, Reggie," answered Granny. "I've been very happy these past several weeks."

Reggie reached out and took Granny's hands in his. "Then why have you been pushing me away?"

Granny opened her mouth to respond, but no words would come out.

"We're not children where love is a game," said Reggie. "I care for you, Nellie. I thought you cared for me, too. The letters you wrote while you were away made me long to see you. Then, when I see you, my heart fills with sadness when we part. You have such an effect on me that I can honestly say that I feel like . . ." Reginald paused, trying to grasp his thoughts.

Oh, no, not the "L" word, Granny thought as she braced herself for what she knew was coming.

"I feel like I'm falling in love with you."

Granny closed her eyes briefly, then reopened them when she heard several intakes of breath coming from the other room.

"There have been some developments, Reggie," began Granny as she released her hands from Reginald's grip. She could hear him exhaling loudly.

"That wasn't the answer one hopes for when they declare their love."

Granny could hear Reginald's disappointment. "I can't talk about this right now." She turned to walk away, but Reginald's next words stopped her in her tracks.

"Is there someone else?"

His tone wavered, and it killed Granny to hear the hurt in his voice. She took a deep breath and turned around. "No—and yes!" Granny wasn't sure how she was going to tell Reginald about Harold, but she knew it had to be done. "Do you remember when I said I was a widow, and that my husband died on an assignment?"

A look of uncertainty crossed Reginald's face. "Yes, what about it?"

Granny took a deep breath and released it. "My husband may not be dead after all."

There was a long, agonizing silence. Reginald's features were full of surprise, shock, disappointment. "You know this for certain?"

"No, not exactly. I haven't seen him or heard from him or anything. It's more like speculation, not actual factual information. But it got me thinking. If it's true, then you and I dating each other wouldn't be appropriate or ethically correct. I mean, I'd still be his wife if he showed up here unexpectedly. And I deeply love him."

Reginald smiled slightly and shook his head. "I see what you're doing. It's a stretch, even for you, but you're trying to push me away with this resurrection business."

Granny, taken aback by his total disbelief, shook her head emphatically. "No, Reggie. I'd never use Harold as an excuse to push you away. I care for you, too."

Reggie's smile warmed, seeing the sincerity in Granny's eyes. "I'm sorry! I can tell you're really concerned about this." Reggie paused before continuing. "Harold was pronounced officially dead by Scotland Yard. You've been a widow for five years. In all that time aren't you supposed to move on with your life?"

44

Granny wasn't sure how she should answer that question. After the loss of Harold, she had moved on. But with his death in question, was she now being fair to Reggie?

"We're going away for a few days on a case. We can talk about this upon my return. I can't concentrate on it right now."

Reginald was upset, desperately searching for an argument that would sway Granny. He clearly didn't want to lose her.

"How about I go with you? I really want to spend some time with you. How far away is the case?"

Granny looked at him with concern. "It's in the Lake District near Derwent."

Harold brightened. "Good, that's only a four to five hour drive. I'll drive everyone in my van and we can talk."

Granny began to shake her head.

"Please, Nellie. You can't change the course of history based on unproven information. You know that. You're a detective for goodness sakes. Look, I promise I won't interfere with your case. I'll keep my distance and let you and your team work your magic."

Granny was determined to say no, but her feelings for Reggie caused her to change her mind, that and the fact that he was in law enforcement and might be of some help. Added to that was the concept of not having to drive herself.

"Oh, all right, we're going to leave in an hour. Go home and pack. Meet us back here then."

At that shocking pronouncement, Max and Mia burst back into the room. "He's coming with us?" said Max.

Reginald smiled broadly, held up his pointer finger and headed for the front door. He opened it, reached out into the hallway and rolled in his baggage, grinning broadly. "It's already done. I'm ready to go when you are."

Granny narrowed her eyes, obviously suspicious. "Seamus wanted to make sure he stayed in the loop didn't he? That sly dog," whispered Granny as she shook her head. "You're assigned to be our liason?"

"But, Granny," said Mia.

Harold, still grinning, ignored Max and Mia's protests. "I'm a detective inspector for the Criminal Investigation Department (CID), the most experienced and medaled in my ranking. Who did you think they'd assign to you? Some no account rookie who'd do you more harm than good? I told you what I did for a living. You said it wasn't a problem."

While Max and Mia stood open mouthed at this, Granny shook her head. "It's not!"

"I know I didn't mention it to you in Las Vegas or in our letters when you went to the Riviera Maya, but I was honest with you about my career, just as you were forthright about yours as a detective. You had to have known our jobs would one day cross paths. What you and your team do isn't exactly a secret around Scotland Yard. There's a history there—a lot of it. Your son and daughter-in-law are detectives there as well and have built quite an impressive resume for themselves. They're good at what they do, as are you and your team."

"And you being Seamus's brother probably gave you no pull whatsoever in you being here, right?"

"My brother might have had a few words with the detective chief inspector about it. They're friends. But to be honest, he knows how I feel about you. He also knows that I'm the most qualified person for the job."

"And Harold? Did he tell you about Harold and our discussion today when I went to the Yard?"

Reginald shook his head. "He mentioned it, but he thought it better that I hear details from you. I haven't spoken of it before, Nellie, but I worked with Harold on many cases. I'm also torn about this. I knew him for years, though Harold was always a private man when it concerned his family. This was not a planned relationship. I had no way intended for this to happen, but it did. After we met in Las Vegas, I knew I had to get to know you better. I was . . . smitten. No one's prepared for cupid's dart. I sure wasn't prepared for my feelings for you. Nellie, you're an amazing woman and it's high time someone made you believe it."

The look in Nellie's eyes softened in the wake of his sincerity.

"I'll stand by you, Nellie. I'm not going anywhere. As I said, I'm in love with you. If Harold ends up being alive and shows up, we'll deal with it then. It's been five years, Nellie. I really think you're getting yourself worked up over nothing, but I understand. Actually, I applaud your honesty and loyalty. But until I see Harold for myself, I'm going to continue seeing you. I won't deny us a chance at happiness because of hearsay."

Granny scoffed at Reginald, her features full of mock disdain.

Reginald's tone quieted as he thought of another way to approach the situation. His gaze took in Max and Mia now for the first time. "Look, your team and Scotland Yard are working together on this case. I'm the liaison between you and them. I usually consider these kinds of situations to be nasty, poisonous, but—it's you. I'm willing to make an exception. And I might come in handy, Nellie. I do have skills, just like you, skills that I have honed over my career and that have earned my position. But, concerning Percival Peacock, we know your team will have the advantage. Your code and puzzle solving is amazing which is why Percival asked for your help and why the Yard okayed the case."

Granny knew she had been given no choice, which was probably Seamus's plan all along. She glared at Reginald for trapping her, but then turned around, hiding a smirk. In fact, she loved a man who took charge. And, if she dared admit it, she was in love with Reginald, too.

"Team!" Granny called, her voice solid and firm. Morris joined Max and Mia in the living room.

"Granny?" asked Mia.

"Pack. Be ready to leave in one hour. Reginald will be driving us to Derwent."

The trio exchanged looks and exhaled breaths, before ducking out to get ready.

"I don't like it," said Max as he and Mia climbed the stairs.

"Well, there's that one big advantage," said Mia.

"Yeah? What's that?'

"We now have half a chance of getting to our destination alive. Granny's not driving."

FIVE

AT THE TAIL END OF THE HOUR, all equipment, clothes, backpacks, snacks, and whatever else the Crypto-Caper team felt they needed, was packed in the back of Reginald's van. As Granny went through a mental list of everything, Morris brought out a unique looking flashlight.

"What's that?" asked Mia as she stood by the kitchen counter alongside her brother.

"I've been reading about Percival Peacock and how he loves to hide information, but he does so ingeniously in the most obvious of places. I wanted to be prepared for what was ahead so I found an Ultra Violet LED black light flashlight. Actually, I created this little masterpiece. There's a black light flashlight for each of us to add to our backpacks. It is water-resistant with a high-strength aluminum case. It has a rear toggle for easy on-off switch for continuous or hands-free use. If you press a concealed button on the underside of the handle the black light will switch off and convert to a regular flashlight. It will save us from having to carry more than one flashlight. Now, the black light fluoresces at distances over twenty feet in darkness with an unbreakable bulb." Morris held up the flashlight and showed it to Mia and Max. "Just as a warning, LED radiation can damage eyes so I'm also packing goggles for each of us. We'll be safe using it even without the goggles, though. Just don't shine it in someone's face or anything."

"What can black lights see that an ordinary flashlight cannot?" asked Mia.

"Well," began Max as he glanced around for a prop. "Let's say these letters that Percival sent had a black light reactive invisible ink on them somewhere. Can I use this, mate?" Max asked Morris, who handed him the flashlight. Max then turned off the kitchen light and drew the curtains, which greatly darkened the room. "Now, all we would have to do is shine it on the paper. If it had black light reactive ink, we'd be able to see the invisible ink." Max shined the light on the backs of Percival's letters. "See, there's nothing, but if there were—" Max stopped. He'd noticed numbers now visible and glaring brightly up from the paper. Mia and Morris had seen them, too.

"No way!" whispered Morris. Before their eyes was a column of several numbers.

Max whispered, "Mia, can you write these down? Quickly!"

Mia scrambled for her notepad where she created a new section for this case. She carefully scribbled down each number set as they appeared.

1-2-21	1-7-17	1-10-37	1-13-24
1-3-10	1-8-22	1-11-22	1-13-33
1-5-39	1-8-38	1-11-32	2-1-9
1-6-24	1-9-11	1-12-30	2-1-29
1-6-35	1-9-38	1-12-39	2-1-35
1-7-2	1-10-15	1-13-15	2-2-9

2-2-15	2-9-16	2-11-44	2-19-32
2-2-29	2-9-27	2-12-22	2-20-4
2-2-32	2-9-37	2-13-17	2-22-25
2-8-32	2-11-5	2-14-2	2-22-43
2-9-1	2-11-37	2-16-3	2-23-2

"What do these numbers mean, I wonder?" said Max.

Mia, though, knew exactly what the numbers meant. "It could be an Ottendorf cipher . . . that's a book cipher. In the last few cases we've been dealing more with Substitution ciphers where all we had to do was substitute one letter of the alphabet for another. This is much harder than that. The reason is because these numbers reference a book."

"What book?" asked Morris.

"Well, that's the problem. Without knowing what book Percival was referring to, this cipher is all but impossible to solve—and useless," answered Mia.

"Does the cipher have to be referenced to a book?" inquired Max.

"No! The creator could use many things—a newspaper article, a magazine, an advertisement, or even just a letter or series of letters—whatever is agreed upon by the creator and the receiver of the cipher. That's what makes an Ottendorf cipher so difficult to solve. Without knowing exactly what was used . . ." Mia trailed off when she stared at the pages on the counter. She was getting excited and pointed at them. "It could be . . . just maybe . . . I bet Percival's letter to us is the key to the cipher." Mia quickly snatched up the pages and flipped them over so Percival's letter was showing. She glanced down at her notepad and looked at the numbers.

"Okay, this is how an Ottendorf cipher works. There are three numbers here separated by dashes. The first is 1-2-21. All the first numbers are either a one or a two, and there are just two pages to the letter. The first number, then, refers to the page number. The second number refers to which line down the page, while the third number refers to which letter on that line. So, when looking at this number pattern and comparing it to Percival's letters the number one stands for page 1."

Mia put her index finger on the first page. "Now, the second number, 2, stands for the second line down the page." Mia's fingers slowly moved to the second line down the page. Max and Morris were watching intently. "The number 21 stands for the letter on that line." Mia began to count the letters on the line until she came to the twenty-first one. "The first letter to the cipher is 'O.'" Mia wrote down the letter on her notepad behind the first grouping of numbers.

"I see how this is going," spouted Max enthusiastically.

"It's going to take forever to solve," added Morris glumly.

"Luckily, we have a long drive ahead of us. Just out of curiosity, shine the black light on the other page." Max grabbed the letter that Percival had first sent them originally telling them about the Globe Theatre and shined the black light on the back of it. An all encompassing picture of a horse covered the page, looking fierce and imposing. He then shined the light on the front. Almost etched on the entire front of the paper was a picture of a dragon. It was tall and beasty looking. Fire flew out of its mouth as his claws grabbed menacingly in front of it.

"What are these pictures supposed to be used for?" asked Morris. "Are they part of the Ottendorf cipher?"

"We have pictures of a horse and a dragon," said Max. "I'm not sure what these mean yet, but if I know Percival, they mean something important to us. We'll need these pictures to use on the case."

Max's observation caused Mia to think. She was in her element. She reached into her backpack and pulled out the map key for the motifs on the Globe Theatre gates, which she had tucked inside a folder. She then quickly scanned down the page on each side of the gates. Mia raised her face briefly, her eyes sparkling like diamonds.

Max caught a glimpse of her excitement. "What is it?"

"I wondered if there was a motif of a horse or a dragon on the gates?"

Max narrowed his eyes in thought, not quite sure what the connection might be. "Is there?"

Granny breezed into the room. "Everyone ready?"

"Bring all papers with us," said Max. "We'll have time in the car to think about it and look things over."

Mia scooped up the papers and tucked them into her backpack as Granny finished with her usual perusal of the apartment. She tossed a few things to each of them, and Max and Morris grabbed a few other items to add to their backpacks.

"Let's go!" Granny waved the team out into the hallway. Sure they'd left nothing behind, Granny closed the door and locked it. When everyone was away from the apartment, heading towards the secured stairs, Morris slid aside a small secret panel just right of the door and tapped in a security code. He breathed easier knowing their valuables were safe. If anyone tried to enter without a key, a silent alarm would go off, alerting the guards inside the building. When he had installed it months before and tried it out, the guards had showed up in less than five minutes. Morris let out a deep breath and smiled, then raced to catch up with his team.

SIX

THE CAR RIDE TO THE LAKE DISTRICT was uneventful, though lengthy, which was considerably better than the possibilities had Granny attempted to drive. The farther they headed north the less traffic they saw, but the landscape was more beautiful. Like most countries, England's landscape was varied. There were the cities, of course, but in the country one could see fields and plains, hills as green as emeralds as they rose and fell, some with great height. In the summer the beauty of those hills could revive the spirits of even the most depressed or lost soul. However, the hills just then were turning brown and bare, its summer beauty going dormant until spring, leaving a starker kind of beauty or line and mass.

The north country had the waterfalls that could inspire poetry, and lakes and, certainly, mountains to capture the eye. The Lake District was made up of lakes surrounded by mountains. The best way to see the Lake District under more relaxed circumstances was walking it. Though the Crypto-Capers knew they'd be doing their fair share of walking, what they needed to do right now was drive to Keswick. Once there, they would have to walk to the Derwent Water, and then go by boat over to the island.

During the first few hours, most of the passengers slept. It was their training. They never knew what to expect on a case or how long it would take them to solve it, so getting enough rest was essential. On the second half of the journey, Mia began to decode the first part of the message. It took her patience and a lot of time, but she did it. It said, "Only trust Steven." Mia relayed the message to the rest of the team.

"Who's Steven?" asked Reginald, glancing at Mia in his rearview mirror.

"I don't know. In his letter Percival explicitly says not to trust anyone. Why would he then tell us to 'only trust Steven'?" answered Mia.

"Because, he's sending us help," replied Max, his right hand cupping his chin in thought. "If someone intercepted this letter and took it from us, they would know exactly what we know. Percival gave us warnings about how not to trust anyone, to beware of other people wanting the diaries, and so on. The only reason he'd send us a coded message about who we *could* trust is because he knows we're going to run into trouble. Before his disappearance, he must have known people were watching his house—watching his every move. Either by design or not, he knows what we're going to have to face. What he's giving us are clues to see past the lies. He wants us to trust the right person. He doesn't want us to trust an enemy."

"But how are we to know the difference?" asked Granny.

"By using the information Percival encoded on the backs of his letters. He put that information there for a reason. We need to discover what that reason is." Max focused his next question on Mia. "Is there more?"

"Yes, I only solved the first part. Now I'm working on the rest." Mia lifted her notepad and glanced back and forth at the letters on her lap. Max glanced over at Morris who was watching something on his laptop through satellite.

"What are you watching?"

Morris briefly met his eyes. "Believe it or not, I'm watching Percival's house on Derwent Island. No one has entered or even attempted to enter in the past few hours. The island's amazing to behold from above. It's not immense, yet it has tons of trees, giving the house plenty of cover and protection around the edges of the island. The police know that we'll be arriving shortly to help with the investigation. The island's locked down."

"The police in the area have secured the island based upon my orders, Morris," Reginald said. "They were ordered to patrol the grounds and the waters, looking for any lurking intruders. There *should* be a few men walking the premises." Reginald paused for a minute. "Are there?" he asked, his curiosity now peaked.

"Well, no, I don't see anyone on the island or even around it, and there hasn't been for some time. Let me expand my view." Morris paused for a second as he pressed a few keys. "Nope, not one officer is near the island. It's barren."

"Hmmm!" moaned Reginald as he pulled out his cell phone and made a call.

"How far are we away?" asked Max to Granny.

"Almost there, according to the GPS. Another fifteen-twenty minutes. We're on the A66, so it shouldn't be long now."

Mia worked studiously on the puzzle, while Max sat back and watched the computer screen with Morris. As the miles zoomed past, Max and Morris began to see a scene unfold on the computer screen. From a spot behind a group of bushes, a boy rose from the ground out of nowhere. Max straightened and pointed, just in case Morris hadn't seen.

He had, though. "Where did he come from?" Morris was already zooming in. It was hard to get a good look at the boy or the ground near his feet. The boy was keeping himself hidden well behind the limbs of the bushes so that no binocular held by the police would detect him. And he never looked up towards the sky, so Morris couldn't see his face by satellite. With bushes surrounding the boy, it created heavy shadows, so though they could partially see his dark-colored jacket, the color was hard to determine.

Suddenly, the boy whipped out a cell phone and was talking on it to someone. It wasn't a casual conversation, either. The boy began gesturing with his non-phone hand as he talked, waving it dramatically, expounding a bit. Before Morris could triangulate the call to overhear what was being said, the boy was off the phone, his face—what little Morris could see of it—looking a little red and flustered. He shook his head and ran his fingers through his hair. He then shoved the phone into his left pocket, his lips moving quickly as he ranted to himself.

"What do you suppose the conversation was about?" murmured Morris.

"It was about something the boy doesn't want to do," gathered Max. "The question is—what exactly is it the boy doesn't want to do?" Then it happened. The scene in front of them changed turbulently. Though no one was supposed to be on the island, the boy who was somehow there was attacked by someone in a dark jacket—who also should not have been there—who was dressed very similarly to the boy, looked like the boy actually. They fought each other, wrestling around on the ground. Then they disappeared, hidden from overhead view by thick, overhanging branches.

"Where did they go?" whispered Max, and he tried to take over control of the computer to zoom in closer. Morris wrenched it from him with a glare and zoomed in closer to the bushes. They could see nothing. Max and Morris glanced at each other for some time, unsure of what just happened, wondering if they'd imagined this attack.

Max, his thoughts consumed with the events that had unfolded, asked softly, "Any chance . . . any chance this isn't the right island?"

Morris, who Max thought for sure would howl offense, checked his coordinates. "It's Percival's island."

Morris continued to search for either boy.

The road they were on curved, following the surrounding hills, and wound its way down into the small market town of Keswick. They were currently in the county of Cumbria. Along the way, they could see the Derwent River, which entered at the southern end and exited at the lake's northern end near Keswick. The river continued to flow northwest through the Lake District to Solway Firth. The Derwent River pooled into the Derwent Water which was three miles long and one mile wide. It also had a depth of about seventy-two feet. There were a number of islands in the lake, the largest being Derwent Island, Lord's Island, St. Herbert's Island, Rampsholme Island, and Otterbield Island. Of course, their attention was focused on Derwent Island, being the one where Percival Peacock's house was located.

The Derwent Water was surrounded by wooded hills with the Lodore and Barrow waterfalls at its upper end. Reginald drove until they reached the car park area that was close to the water's edge and the beach where they would be able to get a boat to take them to the island. Several sites along the lakes shores were National Trust property and were frequented by tourists.

The van stopped, and the team stepped out, taking in the scenic view of the mountains and the water. Even if autumn had drained the landscape of green, it was a sight to behold. The Lake District was a beautiful place and was cooler than the surrounding areas, cooler certainly than London. Dustings of snow already frosted the tops of some of the mountains and fells. The breeze was light, thanks to the mountains shielding them.

The team layered up, putting on hats and gloves. After breathing deeply of the fresh cool air, the team turned their attentions to their own duties. Morris, his laptop encased, took a few other pieces from the equipment bag, putting them into his backpack. Max slung his backpack over his shoulders. Mia did the same, as did Granny. Instead of having a backpack, Reginald transferred a few things from his bag and put them into his medium-sized fanny pack, leaving his heavier suitcase with his fresh clothes in the vehicle.

"All set?" asked Reginald as he closed the door to the van and locked it.

"Yes," replied Granny, looking quickly at her team to be certain. As the group walked towards the beach, Granny asked Reginald about the conversation he had on the phone.

"The officers were called away because of another disturbance in the area. That's why the island was unattended. But now . . ." Reginald pointed at a jetty boat patrolling the chilly waters around Derwent Island. "There they are!" The jetty boat, which was more of a passenger ferry, began to cruise towards them. It slowed as it neared the beach then coasted until it reached the dock. Once there, one of the police officers wrapped a rope around a metal post to secure it.

"Good afternoon, Detective Inspector!" one of the men shouted. Reginald nodded in reply as he helped everyone step into the boat. He then hopped in himself. The rope was untied, and off they went.

"Good afternoon, constables," volunteered Granny, observing their rank, as she moved to sit on a cushion in the back of the boat.

"What news do you have for us?" barked Reginald as he took charge, his confident and stern disposition emanating like heat from the sun.

"There was a street brawl. Those are few and far between around here. Why it wasn't stopped before we arrived was beyond me. I mean, the people just stood around and watched as blokes pounded on each other as if they were starved for entertainment."

"It was meant as a distraction," concluded Max, looking steadily at the officer.

One nodded. "We believe so, too. But a distraction to do what? Pull us away from the island? We surveyed the grounds when we returned. No one can enter into that house and there was no one on the grounds."

"You are wrong on that point, officer," interjected Max. "My team and I observed two boys on the island while you were away. We were watching the island via satellite. What the boys were doing or what they were up to on the island—we don't know. But we do know they were there hiding behind some bushes. They also

61

THE PEACOCK DIARIES

disappeared from our view. The undergrowth on the island is very thick. So, something is going on that we don't know about."

The officer thought for a moment. "Well, that's puzzling. We searched every inch of that island, including through the shrubbery in front of the house and the thick woods all around it. We saw no one."

The constable turned towards his partner steering the boat and whispered something, causing the man to laugh slightly.

Mia couldn't help but comment. "Don't worry, constable, we're here to help you, because, unlike you and your men, we're excellent at solving puzzles. We'll figure out what's going on and save the day for you."

The constable turned towards Mia, his eyes full of contempt. Mia glanced away, but Max met the gaze head on, his features firm as his own arrogant smile rose to his lips. This time the constable looked away.

From the jetty, the house could not be seen. The towers of various coniferous and deciduous trees blocked their view. The house was certainly protected, not only from the weather, but from intruders as well. No one would know that a house even existed on the island because of those trees. It looked like a tangled woods. The air over the water was bone chilling, and Max was surprised the waters had not iced over even though the warmth of the earth still lingered in the surrounding fells that secluded the area.

The island's dock led to a curtain of trees and bushes covered in frost. As the jetty boat docked and everyone stepped off, Max and Morris led the way as they glanced around them cautiously. The shrubbery was even thicker than they thought. Max had expected a path to twist through the overgrowth, but

62

they didn't come to a tree-lined path until well away from the lake. Branches had to be held so as not to whip into the faces of the person just behind. It was slow going. They walked a ways before the path finally opened up and the house mysteriously revealed itself. As it did, the rear of the island looked immense, a series of heavily wooded hills. Before they could continue their walk, they heard a noise behind some undergrowth to their left. Reginald and the constables were the only ones who carried weapons, and they immediately moved in front of the Crypto-Caper team ready to protect them. The disturbance in the woods continued.

"This is Detective Inspector Reginald Jaffrey. Whoever's behind there, come out before I shoot," called out Reginald, his hand holding tightly to his sidearm.

The crashing about stopped.

"I'm warning you," said Reginald in his deepest, most threatening voice.

It didn't take long for two boys to push their way out from behind the bushes and overhanging branches. One shoved the other, and that boy almost fell against Reginald's feet. He turned on the ground and kicked up at the other boy, hitting him in the leg. Before the boys could continue their brawling, Reginald yelled at them to stop.

Clothes torn, face and hands streaked with dirt and the green from smashed leaves, one's nose a little bloody, the boys stood up and stared at the group, out of breath and still angry. They were about the same height, five-foot, six inches tall. They were both thin with short golden-brown hair, but one had chocolate brown eyes and wore a thin navy-blue jacket. Though his features were tan from the sun, his lips bluish from the cold. He shivered and stood hunched. The other boy had bluish-green eyes that glistened like the sea in summer. He wore a forest-green jacket and had the beginnings of a golden-brown mustache above his upper lip. He had something in his pocket that his right hand was protecting when he had sprawled on the ground. Circling his wrist were two bracelets made of smooth bands of Petoskey stone. The boy with the navy-blue jacket spoke first.

"I'm Steven Pendleton, Percival Peacock's grandson. I came here to visit my grandfather. We've been planning this visit for months. I don't know what's going on. Granddad didn't say anything was wrong, but I can't get into the house. What happened?" asked Steven.

"There has been an attack on your grandfather," answered Granny gently.

Concern filled both boys' features. Max analyzed their reactions.

"Is he all right?" asked the boy in the green jacket.

"We don't have a lot of information yet, but it seems he's in hiding. I'm sorry, who are you?" asked Granny

Steven pointed. "He's an intruder I caught trying to break in to my grandfather's house."

"I am not an intruder trying to break in! You are!" yelled the boy. He glared back at Steven, his fists clenched. "I was stopping you."

"Yes, but who are you?" asked Reginald firmly as he stared at the boy in the green jacket.

"*I* am Steven Pendleton! Percival Peacock is *my* grandfather. This imposter ambushed me while I was waiting for you."

"Really? We have two Stevens?" said Granny as she looked from one boy to the other, exhaling a deep breath. "This is going to be easy to determine." Granny smiled.

"Actually, it will be." All eyes were on Mia now. "Max, if you could!" hissed Mia as she waved her brother towards her. "In Percival's letter he mentions to trust Steven."

"Yeah, but which one?" he whispered back. "We don't know who's telling the truth."

"Let me handle this. I solved the rest of the clues." Mia walked up to stand in front of the two boys, but not before Max caught up with her.

"Would you mind an indulgence? A quick assessment, if you will?" Max said. Then in a whisper just for her, he husked, "I want to have a little fun."

"Not at all, dear brother, observe away. In the process you might get them to admit something," replied Mia as she glanced firmly at the boys, knowing her brother's capacity for observation and discovering truths.

"Here is the problem, gents. One of you is lying, while the other is telling us the truth." Both boys appeared nervous as Max walked up to each one and took a close and careful look at each of them. His quiet observation was unnerving to the two. They both fidgeted uncomfortably. Then Max sniffed their jackets and walked around them once more.

"Steven with the green jacket, you're from the United States. Your northern accent screams Michigan as does the deer you have embroidered on the fleece you're wearing underneath your jacket. You brought everything you need to keep warm, so you've been here before. Either that or you're just used to the cold

65

and unpredictable weather. I think you're related to Percival. Your eyes are narrow like his but fit your round face nicely. I'd say the relationship goes through your mother's side. You like to take pictures, based upon your keen eye. I'd even go so far as to say that the thing you're protecting in your right jacket pocket is a camera, and there's a cell phone in your left. You also would prefer to wear a baseball cap and carry one with you at all times. If I were to take a guess—knowing the area—you are a Red Wings fan?"

Before Steven Green Jacket could pick up his jaw, Max turned his attention to the other boy.

"You, the other Steven, were not prepared for England's weather, which means you've never been here before. You're from Australia, and, though you're doing a great job of hiding your accent, it's blatant you have one. You don't like the cold, which explains the three pairs of socks you're wearing, and your skin has a nice tan glow about it. So, you're visiting. I'd say flew into the nearest airport yesterday afternoon. Which explains how unprepared you were for the weather and your inadequate apparel. You also have a fear of cats and an aversion to wool, though you do favor yellow cheese and have a penchant for expensive things."

Both Stevens stared at Max dumbfounded as they looked into their pockets, touched their clothing and faces. The officers standing there were in about the same state of amazement.

Pleased, Max stepped back. "Your game now, Mia."

"Thank you, brother." Mia cleared her throat before she stepped forward. "Max revealed much, but not enough. We still don't know who's telling the truth of why you're here. So, I'm going to ask you a few questions. They're harmless, I assure you, quite simple. What's your favorite color?"

The Steven in the green jacket appeared uneasy. He opened his mouth but nothing came out until he cleared his throat. "Emerald green!" he said.

"I don't see how that's relevant," spoke the other Steven tersely now showing his Australian accent.

"Favorite color!" demanded Mia.

"Royal blue!"

Then, smiling, Mia asked, "What's your favorite pet's name?"

The two Stevens glanced at each other. The Steven in the green jacket calmly replied, though dejectedly, "I don't have a pet!"

"What if you did? At least make an effort on this, Steven. How you respond could save yourself from jail. What *would* you name a pet if you had one?" Mia persisted.

Steven Green Jacket thought for a moment, shrugging his shoulders. "I don't know. I fancy dogs. If I had a dog, I'd probably name it Rodeo."

The other Steven, having had time to consider, replied most happily, "Blaster!"

Mia called to the constables. Steven Blue Jacket smiled smugly at Steven Green Jacket.

"Constables," Mia said, "please take the Steven in the blue jacket away. He was sent by the Panther to deter us."

That statement caused pandemonium. Steven Blue Jacket leaped forward at Mia, his expression now twisted in outrage. But, Mia, prepared for the attack, swung her arms, blocking the blow the boy tried to make and hit him squarely in the chest with her right hand, knocking him to the ground. She then placed her foot against his throat.

Granny and Max stepped closer to Mia, ready to help if needed, while Morris held down the boy's feet so he couldn't kick up.

"Who are you?" demanded Mia as she applied pressure to the boy's throat by leaning forward, "And I know your name is not Steven."

The boy pushed against Mia's foot, but she wasn't budging.

"Max, if you would," encouraged Mia.

Max bent down and checked the boy's pocket for identification.

"No!" the boy objected as he fought against Mia's foot.

Undetered, Max pulled out a wallet and opened it. "His name is Asher Montgomery from Victoria, Australia. Oh, I do love it when I'm right," Max admitted smugly.

"Look, mate, let me go, all right," Asher begged.

"Ah, the sweet sound of that Australian accent rolling from your tongue. So, how is our beloved Panther?"

Asher quit his struggling. "He's spewin', and in a very vengeful mood."

"Spewin'?" asked Morris, confused.

Max turned and smirked. "Aussie slang. The Panther's very angry with us." Max then turned around. "And I don't blame him. But he is only getting what he deserves. How does it feel, Asher, to be his new fool of the month? What did he bribe you with to help him?"

Asher's face twisted, and Max realized that the boy had not joined the Panther's ranks by choice. "What does he have over you?" Max asked.

"He has . . . he has my little sister, Ria. He said if I did this for him, he'd free her."

Mia eased up with her foot on his throat, and Morris let his legs go. The boy sat up, now visibly upset. "And what is it that you are supposed to be doing for him, dear?" questioned Granny.

"I'm supposed to find out where this Percival Peacock bloke is hiding and get his diaries." Asher visibly paled as he looked away. "And if I don't . . . if I don't . . ."

"What did he threaten?" asked Morris.

Asher's eyes focused on Morris, tears filling them. "Then he'll use my sister to do a job. He said it'd be highly dangerous. Look, mates, I can't let him do it. It's bad enough he's sunk his claws into me, but to force my sister into a thief's life—"

The constables took Asher's arms and hauled him to his feet. In a moment he was handcuffed.

"Take him away and place him in the nearest jail cell," ordered Granny. "But don't hurt him. We'll confer on how we're going to deal with him. For now, put him where he'll be safe. Oh, and don't allow him any visitors until we can figure this all out. We don't want the Panther getting to him." Granny turned, then spun back. "Also, check him for wires and tracking devices. We must make sure he's telling the truth. We wouldn't want a surprise visit from the Panther. That would be awkward, though certainly not unexpected."

"Yes, detective," answered one of the constables as they started off with Asher towards the jetty.

The group turned their focus to the real Steven. "First, though," said Granny, "for our peace of mind . . . Morris, dear?"

Morris knew what she was asking. He pulled out his laptop and quickly checked the Panther's position.

"He's on the move, but to no great extent. He's still in Australia, but he's in Victoria now instead of Sydney. Asher might be telling the truth. I have some friends down there. I'll have them check out the situation. They can confirm Asher's story and, if it's true, can try to free the sister. They owe me anyway."

With Morris's reassuring words and continued typing on his keyboard, Granny focused her gaze on Steven. "Was Max right in his assessment of you?"

Steven smiled. He lifted a camera from his right pocket and his cell phone from his left. He then slightly unzipped his thick jacket and reached inside, pulling out a baseball cap. It had the red-and-white colors of the Detroit Red Wings hockey team.

"He was indeed." Steven turned to Max as he replaced everything back into his jacket. "I don't know how you knew all that about me, but you were right on. I'm from Michigan. I came here to visit with my Grandfather Percy, but as you can see, he's not here to visit with."

Morris eyed Steven.

"But you knew that, didn't you, Steven?" said Mia. "It would be great if we could dispense with *all* the lies and the games. Let's try something new, like maybe telling us everything you know about what's going on, and the truth mind you, not sugar coated lies. We can see right through them anyway."

Steven stared a moment, then nodded. He took a deep breath. "Okay! As you apparently already know, my grandfather sent me here to help you find the diaries. I wasn't lying when I said I was waiting for you. I can't give you the answers you seek, but I can guide you along the way a little. My grandfather's house is horrifying in ways you can't possibly imagine. I'll navigate you to an extent, but the rest must be up to you. His house is just the start, and it won't end there. I believe you already began the quest in London, yes?"

"Yes! We've the information he left for us."

"Perfect. I trust my grandfather's judgement. I don't know why I doubted your team's abilities, but your little demonstation about me sure quelled those doubts. I hope you keep proving me wrong."

"See, that's better," chimed in Granny.

"What's better?" asked Steven.

"Speaking the truth!"

Steven grinned.

"I've a feeling you don't really want to be here," observed Max, still feeling like they were missing something important.

"Considering I have to protect Grandfather's secrets from a man who's a known murderer, thief, and betrayer, no, I'd rather be almost anywhere else. In my situation, you'd have some resistance, too. The shining light is I'm no longer alone in this. I'm going to be helping the best detectives in the world, in my opinion, to stop him. No others have done what you have done in getting close to the Panther. That man needs to be stopped."

"You still know more than what you are telling us," accused Mia.

"Indeed I do." Steven, looked away. "Indeed I do."

"Why all the challenges?" asked Morris. "Why can't Percival just give us what we need and be done with it?"

Steven walked up to Morris. "As a fellow computer geek, I thought you'd like the challenge," asserted Steven.

"I do—always—but . . ."

"To be forthright, you need to prove your worth . . . to my grandfather. Reputation is nothing if you can't back it up. Understand, my grandfather is the keeper of very dangerous secrets. Someone wants him dead because of what he knows and he knows enough to hurt many people. He can't just reveal what he knows to you. You must earn his trust. He thinks highly of you and your team, has researched all of you, so knows your capabilities. He knows your strengths and weaknesses and he'll play to those. He'll test you, torment you to an extent to test your will, your heart. Will you survive it?" He shrugged. "What doesn't break you will make you stronger, and he needs to know to a very fine degree what you can and cannot do."

"Why put us through this?" demanded Mia.

"Because, he also knows the capabilities of the Panther," said Steven.

"Percival knows the Panther's true identity doesn't he?" said Max, his eyes narrowing on Steven.

"He does! That's the problem. He knows way too much. He also knows that the Panther has tested you, pushed and pulled you to an extent that stopping him is almost an obsession, but it's given the Panther information about you too, maybe given him limits he's already planning ways around. That's what worries Grandfather, why he feels he must also test you. He needs you, and you need him. The Panther's evil plans have just begun. You'll have to endure more than what you have, and it will be painful. How you do in the stressful situations will determine how you will survive against the Panther. These challenges will make you stronger and more solid as a team . . . harder to beat. Don't you want that?" asked Steven.

"Of course," answered Granny.

"What kind of man is he to do this to us?" asked Mia, a hand to her mouth.

"A powerful one! He's a man you want on your side. Grandfather is not a bad man, let me make that clear. He's not your enemy. In fact, he wants nothing more than to be your friend. Believe that as you go through these challenges. But there is a lot at stake. On the other hand, an award awaits you at the end of all this turmoil."

"What's to follow?" asked Granny.

"You'll have to wait and ask him that question yourself," answered Steven.

"We will meet him?" surmised Max.

"Of course, *if* you can find him."

"What are we to do now?" asked Reginald.

"I'm to follow you. So, if you're ready, by all means, we should begin. Lead the way to the house and your first challenge," encouraged Steven, and he let the other members of the group lead the way towards the front of the house.

SEVEN

AS PERCIVAL'S FILE HAD STATED, the house had no front door. It had windows, however, and they glinted from the dark-gray brick of the walls. The house appeared to have three stories with several chimneys on a complicated, multi-level roof. They could see some of the upper floor terraces, but those could not be accessed either.

"How do we enter?" asked Reginald, staring up at the mansion, his hands on his hips.

"That is for you to find out," answered Steven mysteriously. When Reginald glared at him, he shrugged and said, "Look, I'm not making the rules here. Grandfather is."

The group walked from one end of the front of the house to the other, analyzing the possibilities. Morris sat down cross-legged in the grass and opened his laptop. He accessed a program he had installed before leaving, thinking it might come in handy, and began to study the walls, working smarter, not necessarily harder. Once he had it set up, he began walking past the front of the house, making sure his camera was aimed at the house. He watched as his camera's red light scanned every brick along the wall. As he walked by a particular window, Morris paused, checked his information, checked it again, then yelled to the group. "I found it."

When everyone crowded around him, Morris said, "The window just to the right of the door is the door."

They went over to stand in front of the window.

"It's the door, huh?" Reginald said.

"So, how does it open?" asked Max. "I don't see a handle."

Morris announced, "No, there's no handle, but we should be able to access the opening with the right amount of pressure on one of these bricks. Steven, would you care to count ten bricks up and two out from the sill on the left side of the window?"

"I underestimated you," Steven admitted as he counted out the bricks, leaving his index finger pointing at the one he arrived at after the count.

"Push it," said Morris.

Steven pressed the brick and stepped back. After several seconds, stairs pushed out of the wall below the window. Max and Mia climbed the stairs, but before either could touch the window, Morris shouted, "Wait!" He continued to stare at his computer screen. Then they heard a latch unlock. "Okay, now. Push against the window, Max. It should open from your side." Max raised his right hand and pressed against the edge of the window. With a little bit of effort, the window swung into the house. Max turned back and smiled. Granny, Steven, and Morris headed for the stairs. Reginald, however, stood his ground, making no move to join them. The team looked at him questioningly.

Reginald, looking just a little uncomfortable, said, "I have orders to wait by the door to make sure that no one goes in or out without authorization." Granny walked down to him and put her right hand on his arm. Reginald nodded his head down to hers and said softly. "I promised that I'd allow you and your team to work their magic. By all means, love, dazzle me. I'll stand down until needed."

Granny wanted to lean up and kiss Reginald, but she resisted. Instead, she beamed him a glorious smile as he reached for her hand and kissed the back of it, winking at her as he let it go.

Max, Mia, Morris, and Steven waited for Granny to join them. Max breathed deeply, then led the way inside, stepping down three steps just inside the window.

Everything was darkened and still in the house, but the richness and elegance was immediately apparent. The interior of the house was amazing with its light wood floors and lengthy decorative rugs. The furnishings showed classical design. Delicate tables and antiques of every description graced the room and expensive art filled wall space and was displayed on table and mantles. To everyone's relief, nothing looked touched. Nothing showed that anyone but Percival had been there. A light layer of dust indicated that he had been gone a few days. But they saw no evidence that an intruder had searched for the diaries.

Steven started to close the window/door, but was stopped by Reginald, who had come up the outside stairs.

"Leave it open, please!" Reginald said. "If I'm needed, I want to be able to hear and get in quickly."

"No problem!" replied Steven, who then joined the others.

The group took several minutes to walk around and peruse the interior. Though they knew enough not to touch anything, every time they turned, their eyes rested on something else both beautiful and clearly expensive.

"The house seems truly amazing. It has more art than a museum. Percival lives here?" inquired Granny.

"He does, yes. Grandfather does like fine things, and his inventions have funded his tastes. I know the house, though elegant, seems harmless to you just to look at it, but it is an astounding house in ways you can't begin to know. Our journey starts in the library, so, would you follow me, please."

Steven led the way to the library, down a surprisingly narrow hallway on the left. At the door, which was dark, paneled mahogany, Steven waited until they had gathered, then opened the door swiftly, stepping to the side so everyone could enter ahead of him. Again, though the window shades had been drawn, enough light penetrated to let them all see more treasures were shelved here, books of immense age, importance, and rarity.

Morris was the last to cross the portal. As he stepped inside, his mouth open and eyes scanning the laden shelves, Steven wrapped his right arm around Morris's neck, quickly yanking him from the doorway and dragging back. The door slammed quickly shut, and Max, Mia, and Granny were left alone in the room.

"Morris?" yelled Mia. "Morris!" She started beating on the door with her fists. "Steven?"

Max pressed his hand upon Mia's shoulder, then applied enough pressure to get her attention. She turned partially around. He took her arm and had to take a step into the room away from the door. All the while, he was staring at the door. She turned to look, too. The door seemed to disappear right before their eyes, melting away and matching into the surrounding walls. One minute Mia was pounding on mahogany panels, then the mahogany was gone, transformed, it seemed, into painted wall and wainscoting. Padlocks, as if by magic, grew like vines along the perimeter of the room. Chains twisted and twirled up and down the middle of the walls. Though they had thought they were among literary history, the room now contained no books at all and was certainly anything but a library.

"What is this?" sputtered Granny, her eyes wide with wonder at the room's tranformation. "What just happened?"

"This is our first challenge," answered Max with surprising calm, and he immediately started analyzing every crevice and corner of the room.

"Why would Steven take Morris?" asked Mia, anger in her voice. "I thought Percival said we could trust him?"

"Don't worry team, I'm here," Morris said into their ear pieces. "It's a part of the test. You have to understand that Percival is orchestrating everything now. Steven was ordered to remove me. But I'm all right." Then in hushed tones, Morris's voice streamed, "I probably can't talk too much, but Steven just left to take a call. I'll help you as much as I can . . . when I can."

"You'll be able to hear everything we say?" asked Max.

"Loud and clear," replied Morris.

"Where are you?" asked Granny.

"Not far from you. I'm in a room down the hall with video cameras. I can see what you're doing. The videos don't have sound, but I'll be able to hear you through our ear pieces. Don't worry, I have your backs," reassured Morris, then he whispered, "Steven's coming back. Bye."

"Thanks, Morris dear," said Granny. "You made us all feel a little bit better."

Max nodded. Then the lights turned off in the room and the windows disappeared, shutting out all sunlight. They were engulfed in darkness.

"Don't anyone move!" ordered Max as he glanced up toward the ceiling. At first, he thought he saw a light. As he continued to stare at it, he discovered the lights were becoming brighter and brighter. The lights appeared to be stars in a blanket sky, but these stars behaved quite differently. These stars began to move to the right and left, up and down. After several seconds, they were done with their transformation.

A hand brushed Max's arm, and Mia said, "Max, is it me, or did those lights just drift into the shape of a constellation?" Max looked again, and, yes, the stars did seem to create a familiar shape.

"You're correct, Mia, but which one?" As if Max's words created a response, the lights suddenly changed. Though the points of lights, the stars and distant constellations remained visible, the dusky shape of a human superimposed on top of them. Two smaller constellations appeared alongside.

"You're so lucky I aced Greek Mythology," spouted Mia as she gazed up at the ceiling. "The interesting thing about constellations is that each one has a meaning. The majority of them were named after Greek Gods. Our birth signs were named after constellations representing the ones each of us were born under. The Zodiac signs."

"Yes, yes. Thank you for the lesson, but which constellation are we looking at? The three stars in the middle remind me of someone I've read about," said Max.

"The three stars in a row we see in the middle form a part of Orion's belt. The Constellation is of Orion, the Hunter. By his sides are his faithful dogs, Canis Major and Canis Minor. Together they supposedly hunt various celestial animals such as Lepus, the

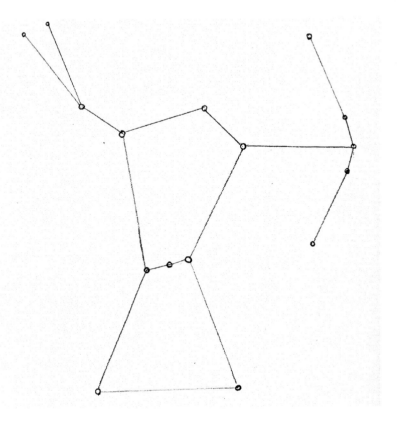

rabbit, and Taurus, the bull," answered Mia.

Max snapped his fingers. "Orion. That's it!"

"Kind of reminds us of the Panther and his henchmen," spouted Granny as she adjusted her glasses. Max and Mia stared at Granny in the ghostly half light in disbelief.

"I don't believe it!" whispered Max, revelation hitting him. He gazed up at the constellation on the ceiling again. "Mia, can you record everything we see and do in these rooms on your notepad?" Mia pulled out her notepad and, after pressing the light on her watch so she could see, wrote down the information they had just acquired. The light, strong enough to light her pad seemed to be swallowed by the gloom of the room.

"What do you think is going on here?" asked Mia as she finished writing and turned off her watch so she didn't waste the batteries.

"The Panther is demonstrated here as Orion," Max said. "He's a hunter of various things in real life. But he's never alone. He always has help of some kind—hence his dogs. We had discussed this earlier when we mentioned that he had many accomplices who risk their lives for him, starting, of course, with his son, Denton."

"Yes, but Orion had weaknesses," said Mia. "He was said to be one of the most handsome of men. But his lust for women was unquenchable and it often got him into trouble. One offense caused his eyes to be gorged out, making him blind. Though he did regain his sight after an oracle told him how, he didn't learn from his mistake.

"He also had one heck of an ego. He was so arrogant and filled with confidence about his own self-worth that he offended the gods. This led to his downfall and why a constellation was named after him. He had offended the gods so badly, they sent a scorpion to kill him,"

"Ah," said Max. "Then the Panther's very similar to Orion. I don't know about the women part, but he's arrogant. Just from our past dealings with him, he's shown himself to be very confident in his own worth. I'll admit, I am too, but not in the same way. If we're reading this correctly, Percival is telling us that the Panther will set the stage for his own downfall, as Orion caused his own pain. It's like a domino effect, really. He takes chances—is rewarded—then punished for them. He can't reach his goal, which is why he has this dependency on us. We have a better chance of reaching it. This is very interesting stuff. The other rooms should prove my theory correct—I hope," predicted Max. Just then the lights flickered.

"We figured out what the constellation means. Now what?" asked Granny as she reached her hand into her handbag and pulled out a flashlight. As she pressed the button, the light splayed differently on the walls than an ordinary light.

"You must have hit the wrong button, Granny. That's the Ultra Violet LED black light," surmised Mia.

"Whoops, sorry about that. I can't tell the difference in the dark." Granny's tone held a hint of frustration. "I just went by feel." As Granny randomly angled the light beam along the walls as she searched for the correct button, the outline of a door developed near the floor.

"Granny!" shouted Mia, quickly moving closer to Granny, placing her hand on Granny's wrist to guide the light beam. The door appeared half the size of a normal door and just below the line of padlocks. Max stepped closer to the eerily illuminated door and touched it. The door was real indeed, but could not be seen in ordinary light. There was no handle so Max pressed against it. It didn't open. On the door appeared a space for something, not sure what, Max looked around. "Mia, could you get your black light out as well and shine it over here please?"

Mia took off her backpack and fished out her flashlight. The flashlights beam soon shone brightly on the walls. To the right side of the door, as if by magic, appeared all twenty-six letters in the alphabet.

"What do we do with those?" asked Granny.

"We spell out Orion's name with them, placing the letters on the door in that space," concluded Mia. "We were put into this room to figure out which constellations we would see. If we get the answer wrong, door may not open. Answer correctly, and we should be able to move into the next room unhindered—I hope."

Max gazed to the ceiling.

"Steven, are we correct in our assumption?"

For a few seconds there was no answer. Max asked his question again, still nothing. "Morris, are you there?"

"Always! We had to tweak the screen. It's so dark in that room that we can hardly see you," Morris spouted angrily. "Wait a minute, here's Steven."

"This is pretty weird, speaking through a head piece, and yet it feels very James Bondish. Look, so far you're on the right track. Keep going. Work it out. Just be cautious."

Steven's warning made the hairs on the backs of their necks stand on end. What was in the next room? The more they thought about it, the more they were unsure if they really wanted to know. Mia breathed deeply.

"All right, Max. Granny and I will hold the flashlights steady while you grab the letters needed to spell Orion's name. You should be able to use the 'O' twice."

Max put on his goggles before walking over to the wall and carefully placing his hand on the letter. As if by magic, the O clung to his hand as he raised it away from the wall and walked over to the door, placing it on the first spot. The letter let go of his hand and settled into its location. To Max it had almost seemed alive. He repeated the action a few more times until all of the letters for Orion's name were spelled out on the door. When his job was finished, Max stepped back, not quite sure what was going to happen next. They watched the letters disappear then replaced with ten more blank spaces.

"What do I spell out now?" asked Max.

"Ten spaces. Spell out Canis Major, then if prompted, Canis Minor. That should do it," encouraged Mia.

Max did as instructed. After spelling out Canis Major, the spaces became blank again leaving ten more spaces. Max spelled out Canis Minor, hoping that would be all he'd have to do. As he stepped back, he watched as the letters disappeared, but this time no blank spaces replaced them. Clenching his fists, Max muttered, "Please work! Please work!" Soon, they all heard a loud unlocking sound echo around the room.

Max stepped forward and pushed on the door. It opened up to another mysterious room. Max led the way. As they each stepped through the threshold, the room seemed even darker and more menacing. No light, no constellations shining upon the ceiling. Mia placed her hand upon her chest as she gazed through the darkness. It revealed nothing. Were they walking into a trap? They were unsure, but once the entire team made it inside of the room, the door slammed shut, locking them in. A loud locking sound seemed to seal their fate.

EIGHT

MIA AND GRANNY INSTANTLY SHINED their light beams around the room. Their black light revealed nothing, so they pressed an underlying switch that converted the black light into a regular flashlight. The light from the flashlight now exposed them to several interesting and unique objects. This room had shelves layered on every single wall around the room. Crowded on each shelf were music boxes, dozens and dozens of them, some simple, some carved with exquisite detail—ballerinas, mothers, children, clowns, and animals. Beautiful porcelain flowers in various shaped baskets. Then there were some wood music boxes, appearing to be antique and very expensive, and silly cheap ones like a little girl might like.

Suddenly, blinds on the other side of the room rotated and opened, allowing sunlight to fill the space. Mia and Granny turned their flashlights off, returning them to their backpacks. Max removed his goggles as well.

"There's got to be a hundred music boxes in here," observed Granny as she peered again around the room, noticing some tall music boxes on the floor. "What exactly are we looking for?"

"I don't know," whispered Max as he raised his hand to tap at his chin.

"Granny," said Morris. "Can you put on your special glasses, please, so I can see what you're looking at? There aren't any cameras in the room you're currently in. Just hearing what you're doing might not be enough for me to help you." Then Morris added, "Granny, you should like this pair of glasses. When I saw them I thought of you."

Granny reached into her handbag, which she had tucked inside her backpack. Mia and Max helped by training their flashlights on the handbag. Granny found the smooth emerald-green hard case, and she let out an, "Ooo." Opening the case revealed a pair of the most stunning glasses she had ever seen. They were bright reddish-pink, reminiscent of a flamingo. The frame was narrow with the sides flaring up like wings. "Ah," said Granny.

She put them on and looked at herself in her compact mirror by the flashlights. "I like these, Morris," Granny crooned as she put her regular glasses in the green case. "They fit perfectly."

"I knew they would." After a few keyboard presses, Morris was able to see everything that Granny was looking at through her glasses. "Good, now pan the room for me, please."

Granny did as all three of them used their flashlights to illuminate what Granny saw, allowing Morris to see the many music boxes.

"Do me a favor, Granny. Raise your watch so it's the height of your chest, with the face of the watch towards the ceiling."

Granny raised her arm in the exact position indicated. Suddenly, a straight red beam shot out across the room. Then it gained in height, the band analyzing every surface.

"This is not good," announced Morris as he stared at his screen.

The words caused Mia's heart to flutter. "What is it?" she asked.

"Well, it's a minor thing, really. I mean, it might not affect anything . . . or it could—"

"Morris," snapped Max.

"Sorry. What you're looking at aren't ordinary music boxes. In fact, I'd say they are not exactly real at all."

"They are holograms?" assumed Max.

"Well, no, I wouldn't say that. Let's just say they're . . . dormant for now, and that leads me to the next conclusion. You better start thinking about how to get out of that room. No hidden panels. That makes me nervous. Look to the left. On the second shelf down from the top you'll see four books. Note the titles."

All flashlights and eyes focused on the shelf. Small movie character music boxes appeared on each side of the four books, almost protecting it.

"Do me a favor and touch nothing," warned Morris, "not even the books for now. Just read me the titles."

Max moved toward the shelf until he stood right in front of the books. "Well, let's see, we have a book titled, *The Music Box*. There is *The Complete Tales of Beatrix Potter*, a collection of all of William Shakespeare's works, and the last book is a collection of Moliere's works."

"Good, now let's see how these fit. Moliere and Shake-speare were playwrights, correct?" confirmed Morris.

"Yes! Shakespeare began his career writing comedies and histories. Then he moved to tragedies and tragicomedies, or what were called romances. Some of his best known works were of his tragedies. The plots were often hinged on some fatal flaw which overturned order and destroyed the hero and those he loved. *Hamlet, Othello, King Lear,* and *Lady MacBeth* have prime examples of these flawed heroes," answered Mia.

"Flaws like what?" inquired Granny.

"Jealousy, a king giving up his power, uncontrollable ambition. In *Hamlet,* which has been discussed more than any other play, Hamlet's fatal flaw was hesitation to act, where in *Othello* and *King Lear,* the lead characters were undone by hasty errors of judgment. Shakespeare turned men's most grotesque desires against them, including greed. In his final period of writing, which was of his tragicomedies, Shakespeare's tone became graver. The endings were of reconciliation and forgiveness of tragic errors, instead of the condemnation of them. Some scholars believed the plays reflected Shakespeare's serene view of life, and that he was more at peace with himself."

"And Moliere?" asked Morris.

Mia said, "Well, Shakespeare acted in some of his own plays, though not all. He had his own company, the King's Men, that performed them. Moliere acted in almost every single one of his own plays, even up to the day he died. His plays were mostly comedies, more humorous then Shakespeare's. Moliere made an art of mocking almost anything. He couldn't stand doctors so mocked them most often, probably because he was sick and saw many doctors later in his life, but he also mocked religion. That got a few of his plays banned from public viewing. As you can imagine, the clergy had fits about them. The only golden parachute that frequently got Moliere out of trouble was the fact that he was friends with the king at the time, and the king absolutely loved his work. The king protected Moliere from the public's wrath." finished Mia.

"What about Beatrix Potter?" Max asked.

Morris jumped in. "Beatrix Potter also lived in England and if my information serves me right, visited this exact house many years ago. That could be where a connection exists for her," answered Morris. "What about *The Music Box*?"

"I can answer that one," slipped in Granny. "I've heard of that title before. It was a classic short film made in 1932. Comedians Stan Laurel and Oliver Hardy were in it. If my memory serves me, the movie was roughly about two men trying to get a piano up a set of impossible stairs. Of course, the actors had fun getting in lots of trouble. Slapstick comedy filled every scene. They made me laugh, that's for sure. It's one of my favorite Laurel and Hardy films. It won an Academy Award for short films."

"Okay, but how does that pertain to anything?" asked Max. "Where's the connection?"

Silence reigned for a few minutes as everyone thought about the information revealed so far. Max suggested, "We need to think differently through this and use some elimination factors. Morris, where did Beatrix Potter live?"

"Oh, she lived near Sawrey in Cumbria right here in the Lake District. She owned, at one time, around four thousand acres, a few cottages and fifteen farms. She was a big conservationist and loved to breed and show Herdwick sheep."

"Really?" asked Mia. "I didn't know that about her. I mean, I've read all her works at one time or another. Mum used to read them to us when we were younger. I've glanced through the stories a time or two since then, but I didn't realize she was a conservationist."

"You said she *once* owned a bunch of properties," began Max. "What happened to them since her death? She died in 1943, correct?" Max had his right hand upon his chin in thought.

Morris divulged, "Now, this is interesting. My research reveals that she bequeathed all her holdings to the National Trust. Truth be told, this island house is also under the protection of the National Trust. That means that it's preserved and no one can tear it down."

"What does The National Trust do again?" asked Mia.

Granny answered that question. "The National Trust works to preserve and protect the coastline, countryside, and buildings of England, Wales, and Northern Ireland. It doesn't cover anything in Scotland, though."

"Why not in Scotland?" asked Mia.

"Because Scotland has its own National Trust." Morris smoothly added, "Currently, the trust owns many heritage properties, including historic houses and gardens, industrial monuments and social history sites. It's one of the largest landowners in the United Kingdom, owning many beautiful spots, most of which are open to the public free of charge. It has the largest membership of any organization in the United Kingdom, and it's one of the largest charities by both income and assets."

"Now, that's interesting," commented Max, moving around Granny and Mia. "What about Moliere and Shakespeare? How could they be connected to Beatrix Potter?"

"They're really not. In his final years Shakespeare lived in Stratford-upon-Avon. He, of course, had quite an illustrious career, but so did Moliere. The difference is that Shakespeare lived in England, Moliere in France. He was a French playwright. They both were friends with the kings of their time. As of today, both their works are well known."

"So, we have two famous playwrights, an author, and actors? Granny, were Laurel or Hardy from England?"

"Stan Laurel was. He was an English actor. He lived, I believe, near Dockwray Square in North Shields in Northumberland. In fact, I believe the idea for the stairs in *The Music Box* was brought about from a set of stairs near where he lived. He moved to California where his career took off with his partner, Oliver Hardy."

"We know the Panther is a playwright," said Max, in his thinking-out-loud mode. "He proved as much in Las Vegas. He directed that play, which, from what I hear, is still a big success. I also remember Morris mentioning that his career had started in England with *After the Taming of the Shrew*, a Shakespeare play twisted and interwoven with comedy, like Moliere. Could they have possibly have been his two favorite playwrights?"

Morris remarked, "As always, Max, your logic is astounding. I think you might be on to something. But there must be another connection than just that. Then again, it could be as simple as that. Shakespeare and Moliere could have been his favorite playwrights, and he copied their style and wit when writing his own plays, yet incorporating life's lessons."

"Which playhouse was the Panther's first play performed?" asked Max.

Silence reigned for several minutes while Morris researched it. "The Globe Theatre. That's ironic," murmured Morris.

Max snapped his fingers. "That was the other reason why Percival had sent us to the Globe—to discover this information. The Globe was rebuilt in 1998, so sometime in the past twelve years the Panther turned into the man he is today. The question we need to ask ourselves is how did a playwrite become a master criminal? What events led up to his decision to go that route?"

"He could have been the Panther years before that, Max," added Mia. "The Panther is a man in his what—forties? Denton is in his twenties. There's much time between them to turn bad. He loves his son, though there's certainly an issue with Denton's competence. Panther made that clear in Mexico. But I think the Panther doesn't quite see Denton's full potential, like most fathers. He's still too preoccupied in his own career to see anything else. He'll see soon enough, though. There's no living mother. Denton had been living alone for years. The police who visited his apartment said there were no pictures of any kind on the walls or in photo albums that would depict someone else in his life."

"What, no past? Denton was clever in hiding it, but it doesn't mean that this didn't all start because of a woman. Denton's mother, perhaps? Or another woman? We're missing something," sighed Max in frustration. "People just don't turn bad. As in Shakespeare's works, we're looking for a fatal flaw."

"Well, we do know there's a connection between Shakespeare, the Globe, and the Panther," inserted Granny. "There's more to figure out."

"What about the other books?" inquired Morris.

"Decoys?" suggested Granny. "This room's obviously filled with music boxes of all sorts. To pick the book which has the name *The Music Box* would be too easily a mistake. Moliere is a French playwright so it is another false clue. The choices are between Beatrix Potter and Shakespeare."

"Possibly! You definitely have a point. Do we have a solution on how to get out of that room yet?" asked Morris.

Mia was on her knees studying the floor. "There is a trap door in this floor. If it takes us to the next room or not is beyond me. It could also take us straight into trouble." As Mia was about to get up, she glanced up and saw a piece of paper on the underside of the shelf containing the books. She quickly rose and walked over to the shelf. Being careful not to disturb or touch anything else, she gently tugged at the paper. It dislodged and Mia looked at it. She showed the rest of the team her prize, then carefully unfolded the worn cream-colored paper. Written on the paper was a quote from something or someone. Mia read it aloud.

"I'll be at charges for a looking-glass; and entertain a score or two of tailors."

"What in the world does that mean?" asked Granny.

Mia glanced at the page, she then laughed. "I know where I've read this quote before. I don't remember who said it, but it's in *Richard III.* But I have seen it somewhere else, too. When mum read to me the different stories written by Beatrix Potter, I saw this same quote as a caption below a picture. It was a part of the introduction for *The Tailor of Gloucester.* Richard III was the Duke of Gloucester in the play."

"Brilliant!" said Max. "Now we know in what town the Panther might have once lived or had a connection to. Gloucester. At one time there was a tailor there. A well known chap. Famous for the unique style in which he sewed. I remember reading about it in the newspaper. The man passed away years ago. That could have been a relative of the Panther. His father, perhaps? Good job, Mia," congratulated Max. Then another revelation hit him. "We have to take a book from the shelf to put things in motion."

Mia's head turned sharply to stare at Max. "That seems like a uniquely bad idea. Are you sure that needs to be done?" Dread filled Mia's voice.

Suddenly, Steven's voice filled the room. "Max is right. You need to activate the next step or your escape route will not open."

"Escape route? That sounds pleasant. Exactly, what are we escaping from?" inquired Granny.

"I can't tell you that," responded Steven. "Just be prepared for anything." There was a brief pause. "I mean *anything!*" The warning wasn't very comforting. Mia glanced at Max who nodded his head to begin.

"Which book should I take?"

"The one you know has the information we seek," advised Granny. While she and Max waited for Mia to make her decision, they readied their flashlights to use as weapons, if necessary. Max then pulled out a small rectangular object that fit right into his palm. At the end of it, near the exact center of the object, appeared to be a red bulb.

"What's that?" asked Granny.

"A new toy from Morris. You have one, too. Perhaps you should get it out. Mia, do the same. We all need to be ready when trouble comes."

From her position, Mia reached into her pants pocket and pulled it out, waving it in the air to show Max she had it.

"Morris showed me how to use it. I was nervous about this place so I've kept it close."

Granny had all but disappeared into her pack, searching for the device. Once she pulled it out, she straightened her hair, then turned it over in her hand.

"Morris showed it to us while you were having your discussion with Reginald," Max said. "It's a laser. When aimed at any mechanical, moving object, it will vaporize it to dust. After hearing the trouble the policemen encountered, Morris thought this might be a great gadget to have." Max inhaled deeply, then exhaled, murmuring, "I hope he's correct."

Granny, Mia, and Max placed their thumbs on the tiny black buttons and pressed them. A bright red line shot out from the bulb. For the next few minutes they played with it, moving the light here and there around the room, then focusing the beam of light on each music box, getting used to the quick movements and angles. Lastly, they practiced the quick flicking of the wrist that some movements required. After feeling confident on how to use the laser, they pressed the soft buttons again, and the red lights disappeared.

Mia held the laser in her left hand while her right poised over the book of her choice, the Beatrix Potter collection. "Are we ready?" she asked.

"Go!" Max ordered and Mia pulled the book from the shelf. As soon as she did, the sound of metal clanging against metal echoed around the room as each music box transformed into a large ten-inch-bodied tarantula. It was hard to believe that even the prettiest looking music box was now replaced by the form of a terrible beast, one with venom dripping from wicked fangs.

"Oh my!" commented Granny, her hand quickly going to her mouth, her eyes wide with surprise. There had to be at least one-hundred tarantulas turning their way. None were directly behind them, but there were several to the sides and certainly in front of them. Max breathed deeply again, trying to remain calm. As he glanced from one tarantula to the next, he noticed that at least six of them had a red tint to them.

"Steven, now would be a good time to help," demanded Mia as she stepped back until she was just a few feet ahead of Max and Granny.

"The only help I can give you is the knowledge that these are biting tarantulas. They will and can jump. Some are harmless, but others contain a poison."

"Let me guess," observed Max. "The red ones contain a poison?"

"Your assessment is correct."

Max shook his head in frustration. He raised his arm, his grip on the laser tightening. He encouraged Mia and Granny to do the same.

"Aim for the red spiders first. Fire at will!" Max shouted and a trio of red beams lit the room as each person aimed it at a red tarantula. As soon as the light hit them, the arachnids immediately exploded, turning into dust. Some tarantulas, seeing their fallen comrades, began to attack, while others went into hiding. One tarantula after another jumped towards the group, the majority of which were caught in a red beam and dissolving into nothingness for their efforts. The number of tarantulas quickly diminished down to ten. But these ten were not going easily. All but one of the red spiders had been destroyed, and that one was hiding.

Mia had the book tucked tightly under her left arm as she maneuvered the laser in her right hand, moving her wrist back and forth, trying to hit a tarantula flying at them. So far, none had gotten close, but now they were coming out of the woodwork it seemed. Before they knew it, a shiny silver tarantula landed on Max's right shoulder. He screamed in pain before he was able to dislodge it and aim his laser directly at the center of it.

Granny was attacked at the same time. Mia turned to help her, but not before destroying the rest of the tarantulas in front of her. Feeling confident she was safe, Mia aimed her laser at Granny's leg where the beast clung tight. She waited for the perfect moment, then shot the laser. It exploded into dust.

When all was clear, Mia smiled, greatly relieved. Max began to laugh, as did Granny, more out of the stressfulness of the situation. Mia's eyes glazing over slightly. Both Max and Granny saw the change.

"What's wrong, Mia?" asked Max. But the answer soon revealed itself when Mia fell to the floor. The book and laser dropped from her grasp. On her back was the last tarantula, the red one that had been hiding. He had bitten Mia, and its poison was seeping through her body. Blood from the bite already soaked through the back of her shirt. Max used his laser to destroy the beast. But he knew it wasn't enough. When it dissintegrated, he yelled, "NO!" his voice tortured as he rushed to his sister's side. Her body convulsed a bit, then went still. He quickly placed two of his fingers to her throat, checking for a pulse. She was still alive.

"Morris, help! Mia's been bitten by a red spider."

Steven replied, though Morris could be heard yelling in the background and throwing stuff. "I have the antidote, Max. You and Granny must move on to the next task. When you achieve that, Mia will be taken care of."

"No, you come save her now!" demanded Max, tears filling his eyes. "Get your bum out here and give her the antidote."

"Listen to me, Max." Steven said slowly, carefully. "You need to leave the room immediately. The door to the room will not unlock until you leave it. Only then can I come in. I have ten minutes to inject her with the antidote or she dies. Your stubbornness will kill her."

During the battle with the spiders, a trap door had opened slightly in the floor. Max noticed it and made eye contact with Granny. He ran his fingers through Mia's hair, then leaned down and kissed her cheek. Granny, who was crying, held fast to Max's arm, urging him to go. They crossed to the trap door.

"Morris," Max shouted, "bypass the system and get in here. Take over. Do something!"

It took several seconds for Morris to respond to the demand. "I promise I'll handle this and do what I can once you leave. She'll live, Max. Go to the next level and defeat it. Beat this game."

"Morris!" Max's indecision held him near his sister.

"Maxwell Sherlock Holmes," ordered Morris, his voice filling with anger. "Finish the job. Get it done at all costs. Isn't that what we were taught?"

"Morris, I beg you, don't force me to leave. We're mates, man—like brothers. Don't let this happen."

Morris's jaw clenched and tears streamed down his cheeks. He pressed several buttons on his laptop, and Mia's body readings popped up. After several seconds Morris's features became firm and unyielding, like a granite wall. When he refocused, he was another person. He was filled with more strength than ever before. He knew what must be done, and knew Max had to play his part. Instead of shouting, which wouldn't have worked with Max anyway, his voice deepened. "Believe in me, Max, like you've always believed in me. Mia's readings are steady—but fading. I love you, brother, which is why you'll go down the blasted hole and finish the job you were meant to do. I'll take care of Mia."

The seriousness in Morris's voice woke Max from his stupor. Without further hesitation, Max walked over to the Beatrix Potter book, which had landed open when Mia had dropped it. Inside the book was hollow. In it was a key. Max snatched the key and tucked it into his backpack. He picked up Mia's notepad, her laser, and her backpack. After stashing those, he moved to the hole in the floor, where Granny waited for him. Max jumped down the hole, dropped several feet until the inside of a tube caught him and slid him away. Granny turned to face Mia a last time, trying not to let emotions dictate her next move, but couldn't help it. "She better live, Steven, or the only person you'll have to fear is me, though I dare say, Max will be no picnic either."

Steven husked, "I'll save her, Nellie. That's why I'm here, just in case this happened."

Granny pursed her lips, shook her head quickly, then jumped into the hole.

As Morris watched, barely breathing, the room turned back into a room lined with shelving, music boxes, and books. The trap door vanished.

Steven bolted from his chair, a small case in hand, and headed towards the door. Morris followed as they ran down the hallway toward a locked room. Steven shoved a key into the lock and turned it. The door opened immediately, giving them access to the room and to Mia, who was lying on the floor. Morris dashed to her side and cupped her cheek in his hand. His fingers then raced to her throat to feel her pulse. It was beating softly, but steadily.

Morris watched anxiously as Steven removed a syringe from a case. It was filled with a yellow liquid. He knelt down and stabbed it into Mia's arm. Morris watched and waited with anticipation. He reached over and cupped Mia's cheek again, his thumb brushing against her cheek. Tears began to roll down his cheeks full force when Mia's eyes opened and she gasped for air. After several seconds her gaze focused on Morris.

"What happened?" she asked, her voice soft and weak.

"You were bitten by the last poisonous spider. Steven injected you with the antidote. I'm going to call Reginald and have you taken out of here. You need medical attention. Can you sit up?"

Mia tried to sit up, but couldn't. She was still too weak. Morris watched her rest her head back down on the floor, her eyes closed. Morris pulled out his cell phone, pressing the buttons rapidly with his thumb. He talked with Reginald briefly, telling him to meet him by the door. Once the call ended, Morris focused his attention on Steven.

"How much time did Mia really have left before the poison would take her?"

Steven swallowed. "The poison is deadly if not treated with the antidote within an allotted amount of time."

"You didn't answer the question."

Steven paused for a few seconds. "What was the allotted time? I may have had less time than what I originally estimated. We cut it close. We could have lost her."

Steven's confession caused Morris's head to nod. He then did something uncharacteristic for him. He struck out with his fist and hit Steven across the face, propelling him backward until he landed on his back on the floor. Steven's howl of pain released the frustration Morris was feeling as he bent down and picked up Mia. Once he had her securely in his arms, he turned to leave, but not before stopping in front of Steven.

"Be more accurate when it comes to defying death. These people are important. You made a careless mistake."

A little angry, Steven looked up, his hand over his cheek. "So you're telling me you've never made a mistake in guiding your team?" Stevens's words were muffled slightly by his hand touching his face, but his tone was not lost on Morris.

"First of all, A, this isn't your team—it's mine, and, B, there's a difference between my leadership and yours. When I run the show from behind the scenes, I have complete control of the situation. You don't have any control. The keeper of that is on the other end of your cell phone." Morris tried to control his emotions but was having a hard time. "We're not puppets here for your amusement. Our lives are not expendable. Think about that the next time the life of one of my team members is in peril."

Though he wouldn't say so, Morris's hand throbbed with pain as he held Mia tighter to his chest, not wanting to drop her. His eyes burned holes through Steven. Morris was livid at the carelessness of the situation. Sure, there'd been times when he put his team's lives in danger, but it was never without a plan to get them out of it. What would they have done if Mia had died? The reality was that each of them accepted and understood the risk involved with each case. Anything could happen to them at anytime—and had. As cold as it sounded, a part of their job was to finish their task, no matter if one of them was down. It didn't mean it wouldn't affect them, but they still needed to accomplish their goal. Mourning would have to wait for later. But fortunately, Mia had a chance, and Morris and the rest of the team were going to cling to that chance. Morris walked from the room, down the hallway to the room with the window/door where they had entered. Reginald was there waiting outside to take her to the nearest hospital.

NINE

THE TUBE CURVED TO THE LEFT, lowered, turned to the right, lowered again, but this time dropping several feet before the tube gently scooped them up, turning to the left one more time before ending. Max and Granny were dumped unceremoniously onto a large sponge cushion in what their flashlights revealed as a basement. All four walls appeared to be made of heavy rock blocks, and the room was damp, a clammy chill seemed to drift over them, making them both shiver. As they continued to examine their circumstance, they were on perhaps a mattress cushion raised off the ground by pallets, which they heard creak and crack slightly when they moved. They could hear water dripping, the sound echoing hollowly throughout the room, but they couldn't find the exact source.

After a sweep with the regular lights, Max suggested, "Try the black light."

Granny heard Max's unhappy tone, and she knew he was thinking about Mia, hoping she was okay. So was she, but she had experience to know such thoughts had to be turned off, shunted to the back of the mind. Granny stepped off the cushion as she switched to the black-light feature, and turned toward Max, the sound of her feet splashing in the water causing Max to turn to her.

"Don't dwell on what just happened up there," she soothed. "We have a job to do. Morris is right, but he's not heartless. Steven has the antidote for the poison and will administer it. Percival might be grooming us, but it isn't to his advantage to kill any one of us. If Morris thought something wasn't right, he'd have expressed more concern. Mia will be fine. Morris will see to it."

Max glared at Granny, anger filling his eyes. "It's amazing to me how you can be so calm about this, about so many things. You're as cold as the winter wind, and as unrelenting. How can you be this way? I know you must feel something about what just happened." Max turned away from Granny, not being able to look at her.

Granny exhaled a deep breath, raising a hand to touch Max's shoulder. He shrugged it off. "It's what has to be done. Blame it on the years of dealing with death and being in this business. But don't think I don't have feelings about Mia's life being threatened. I'm feeling so many things right now that I could explode. If I gave in to that, I'd scream and cry and beat on these damp walls. I'd yell at the top of my lungs, punch something, someone, until I can't breathe anymore."

"Then why don't you? When Granddad died, you reacted in the same manner. In front of everyone, you were cold—somewhat distant and yet ready to press on. But away from us, in the quietness of your room when you thought no one was listening, Mia and I both heard you sobbing, drowning yourself in your true emotions, not fabricated ones put on for show. I admire your strength, Granny, and your courage astounds me. You have no idea how much I look up to you and depend on that strength, not only throughout each case, but in life. But feelings are a part of being human. You don't have to be strong all the time. Family can help be your pillar of strength."

Before Max could continue, Granny interrupted him, slowly raising her hand and resting it on Max's cheek.

"Max, there are certainly times when I'm not so strong. I have fears and doubts like everybody else, which is why I go to church. I often pray for strength. Is it satisfying to know that at times I do break down and cry? I even find it hard when we're on a case and visit a place I know Harold's been. Sometimes that's very hard. I remember the gifts brought back for me and the stories he told. Memories flood my mind so much at times, I'm sure I'm going to drown, but if I did that I know I might lose one of you. I can't allow that. So the feelings have to be set aside, pushed away until I have the freedom to deal with them.

"But I'm not as strong as you think. When we return from each case I have to spend the next few days at the spa where my masseuse can wreak havoc on my body trying to relax me. By the end of a case, I become a bundle of knots and stress because I feel that afflicted. The muscles in my shoulders get wound up so tight in knots that I constantly feel like a pretzel."

Max sighed. "It doesn't please me to know that, but it does show me that what you do is training, Granny. I have to respect that."

Granny leaned over and kissed Max on the cheek.

"I'm the man of the house while Dad is away. Since Granddad passed, that makes me responsible for taking care of you as well as Mia."

"Max, that's not a good place for you to be—"

105

Max pushed ahead. "Let me take the burdens from you and carry them. I know you've been troubled and at times . . . unsure of what's going on concerning family. Let me help you. I know you feel troubled."

Granny removed her hand, tears forming in her eyes. "You're too young to deal with such burdens, and you shouldn't have to, though I do know many responsibilities are thrust your way—more than other boys have to deal with—and you handle them beautifully. You're the leader of this team, not me. That's never been in question, and you have your dad's strength in you. If you feel you need to be the man of the house while my son's away, I concede that, but my burdens are mine alone to carry."

"What about Granddad's possible resurrection from the dead? Must you bear that burden alone? We're family. I should also bare the burden."

Harold had been on Granny's mind for some time. Even though she tried to be careful, she knew that her worries and doubts showed and, therefore, spilled over onto her grandchildren.

"I loved Harold, Max. You know that. But after all these years, I feel I have a right to move on. This news about him possibly being alive has filled me with hope—and yet dread. I love Reginald now too, and he loves me. It's nice, for a change, not to have to be responsible for everything. He makes me feel special and adored, and I haven't felt that way in quite some time. I'm filled with laughter again. I hope you can understand that. I don't want you to bear me ill will because of my decision. I'm not betraying your granddad's memory, I assure you."

Max smiled in full force now, the whiteness of his teeth shining brightly in the gloom. "I just want you to be happy,

Granny. Mia and I don't judge you for your relationship with Reggie. We want what is best for you, and if Reggie happens to be that, then we accept him into our family. We will trust him—no questions asked. Don't worry about what we feel. We'll support you in your choices no matter what."

Granny beamed her pride. She had underestimated Max, thinking he wasn't mature enough to understand, but the truth was he understood perfectly. Granny would remember that in future.

"I could always count on you, Max." Granny paused before continuing. "But concerning this other matter, I need you to understand that it'd solve nothing for me to break down whenever something wrong comes my way. I must be strong to be ready for the next thing. This you will learn in time. Yes, I'll admit that, professionally, I've become hardened over the years like a rock. But that's professionally. Your parents, too, have toughened up over the years. Believe me when I say that you'll have to do the same if you're going to survive in this business. Our job is tough, demanding, and, at times, physically exhausting. You know this. We sacrifice a lot. But I've learned that our feelings cannot and should not drive us into making mistakes, possibly more serious mistakes. That could cost us so much more than just our lives."

Granny made sense. Max understood everything she had said, and he knew he had to accept it. He loved being a detective. It made him feel intoxicated and powerful. There was nothing better in the world than being a detective and solving a crime no one else could solve and helping people in the process. Max never considered that what he did was a job—to him it was more of an adventure. He was young, and at the moment, his feelings did drive him. He knew he had to learn from Granny's example.

"You're right, Granny, as always. I can't let my feelings rule my actions. Until I hear confirmation from Morris about Mia's condition, I'll remain strong and focused on the problem at hand. This case. Shall we continue?"

Max's words of acceptance made the room feel lighter. He certainly felt better after expressing his feelings and coming to terms with them. Granny pressed the button on her flashlight causing the light to switch to UV. She then slowly waved it around the room.

"How you know these things, Max, I will never know," admitted Granny. Her light beam rested on a large rectangle on the wall. It appeared to be the image of an aquarium, four feet tall and three feet wide. The bottom of it was a foot from the ground. Pictures of various kinds of fish and coral had been drawn inside the rectangle with florescent paint. To the left of it was a cryptogram.

Max opened Mia's backpack, looking for her notepad. She had placed it in a protective waterproof covering. The plastic held her pad and a pen. Max glanced through the pages for some help. On several Mia had written down clues and information about the case thus far, the solution to the Ottendorf cipher and other notes. Max wrote down the cryptogram on the pad, then began solving it using the partial cipher key she had created. It took Max several minutes to work the cryptogram out, but once he did he looked up and smiled at Granny.

$\overline{O\,H\,B}$ $\overline{G\,E\,Q}$ $\overline{H\,X}$ $\overline{C\,K\,Q}$ $\overline{E\,W\,F\,K\,C}$ $\overline{C\,E\,G\,Y\,N}.$

$\overline{N\,Q\,Q\,I}$ $\overline{F\,H\,W\,X\,F}.$ $\overline{C\,E\,B\,M\,C}$ $\overline{O\,H\,B\,E}$ $\overline{W\,X\,M\,C\,W\,X\,Y\,C\,M}.$

"That's encouraging." Max read to Granny what the cryptogram said.

Granny exhaled a sigh of relief. The words were indeed encouraging. Max closed Mia's notepad and put it into his pocket. The duo moved closer to peer closely at the rectangle. Inside, near the back of it appeared to be a cave of some type. It was as if they were looking at a painting in 3-D.

"What do we do, walk through it, you think?" asked Max.

Granny shrugged. "There's only one way to find out."

She and Max walked close enough to the wall to touch it. Max reached out to an area outside of the rectangle. It felt damp, cold, just a wall. It was different when he reached inside the brightly glowing UV lines of the rectangle. He didn't touch wall, didn't encounter the cold stone. Instead, his fingers seemed to pass right through what his eyes told him was solid stone wall.

"That is so idiosyncratic, yet brilliant at the same time," commented Max, thoroughly impressed with what Percival was able to accomplish. The lengths the man went through to conceal information. Granny and Max glanced at each other before both ducked through the imaginary portal. It indeed led them into a cave. The coolness of the cave washed over them, like the chill of a freezer opened on a hot, humid day and a roil of frosty air escaped. With each step they could feel the hardness of the ground below them change from glacial compact rock to soft and forgiving sand. They both glanced behind them, seeing the stone wall they had seen without the black light, and the UV light showed nothing different. There was no trace of a doorway, no way, therefore, for them to return. It had disappeared.

"I guess we can't go back," observed Granny with a shake of her head.

"I hope we made the right decision in walking through that wall, then," whispered Max.

"I'm sure we have." Granny's voice sounded confident.

They noticed water covering half the floor space. Though they couldn't see an outlet, Max and Granny knew one had to exist. Max surveyed the sand and noticed prints in it that weren't theirs. They were oddly shaped. Max studied them.

"Percival came this way, but he was wearing his diving flippers." The prints led to the water's edge where they vanished.

"He's leading us to him," deduced Max. Then he paused. He thought over Granny's words a minute, doubt suddenly clouding his thoughts. "Are we positive these are his prints? They could be someone else's. An enemy, perhaps?"

Granny shook her head, shrugged, then laughed briefly. "I have a feeling that, if Percival booby trapped everything else in his house to protect the information of the diaries, this is most likely no different. He hasn't made it easy for us so far, and I expect that's only going to get worse. The most comforting part of this information is that no enemy would know all that we know." Granny tilted her head to the side as she shined the black light on the walls and ground in front of them, seeing if there were anymore secret messages. Sure enough, they discovered a cryptogram on the wall.

"I love it when I'm right," bragged Granny. "Would you write the cryptogram down and solve it, please, dear?"

Max wrote down the cryptogram. He greatly appreciated how much work Mia already had done for him. She definitely carried her weight in the group, and she was much better at solving puzzles than he was.

V H A A H D   C K Q   G E E H D M.   C K Q O

D W A A   F B W R Q   O H B   C H   C K Q

X Q J C   Y K G A A Q X F Q.

Max studied the letters from the previous cryptogram and filled in what he could from the cipher key. He then used the key to solve the new cryptogram. It took him about fifteen minutes to complete it. He knew Mia would have solved it in ten. Max read the cryptogram to Granny.

She nodded. "Well, I guess we keep going then."

As they glanced around the room, Max spotted scuba gear in a corner. He rushed over and studied it.

"There are only two sets of gear here. Percival planned for Steven to snatch Morris away, and, apparently he was counting on one of us being taken out by the previous room either by force or injury."

Anger filled Max's voice, but instead of letting his emotions take control like before, he closed his eyes, took several deep breaths, and refocused again on the gear. "We should put it on. It's obvious that he wants us to go into the water."

"Yes, but what are we looking for?" asked Granny.

"I don't know, but we'll find out soon enough," answered Max confidently. He then handed the larger wetsuit to Granny. She began to put it on over her clothes. Max did the same. The suits fit nicely and were the exact sizes for them, which was odd if one didn't take into account the kind of person Percival was. They felt like a second skin. At Max's feet lay a large handheld candle- powered spotlight.

Max had seen them before in hunting magazines. Its lens was not clear, which made Max believe that it would expose any florescent light under the water. The spotlight was encased in tough durable, waterproof dark plastic. Granny and Max spent a few minutes taking a selection of things from their backpacks, then shut the packs carefully. Then they pressed a seldom used button near the top of each backpack that created a hard covering around each one making them waterproof. They put them around their tanks. Max had removed the key and some string from his pack. He threaded the string through the hole at the end of the key and tied it. Once secure, he put it around his neck. He put Mia's notepad and laser in plastic cases in the event they ran into anything mechanical. They checked their gear before strapping the oxygen tanks on their backs. Max lowered his mask over his eyes, adjusted it accordingly, then slipped the mouthpiece into his mouth. After breathing deeply and calmly for several seconds to get used to the air in the tank, Max picked up the spotlight and waved for Granny with his other hand to follow him into the water.

The water felt cold even through the suit. Max walked straight in until the ground gave way. Then he started swimming down into deep water. He swam toward the murky bottom. Granny swam close behind. Max saw a distant light, pointed at it, then swam towards it. He came to a tiny round hole the size of a pea, which looked oddly placed in a gigantic stone barrier. There was no exit. Someone had blocked up the passage, and there appeared to be no escape. Confused, Max looked at Granny and pointed to the surface.

Granny nodded and pushed off from the ground. Max followed her. Once they surfaced and were treading water, they removed their mouthpieces so they could talk.

"What do we do now?" asked Granny.

Max lifted his mask and studied the wall in front of them. He then adjusted the spotlight in his grip. A revelation came to him. "I'll be right back, Granny," he said. Max replaced the mouthpiece, then lowered his mask back over his eyes. An idea filled his mind he couldn't shake. As he swam back down toward the rock wall he shined the spotlight, revealing a type of puzzle. In front of him, drawn in florescent paint, were the planets in the solar system. Below it was a cryptogram.

W̄ GŪ XHC G FHR HE FHRRQMM,

ZBC W GU MCWAA QJCEGHERWXGEO.

Max memorized the coded word segment, then went up top to write the cryptogram down in Mia's notepad. Granny took over that chore. Max would rise to the surface, telling Granny the coded letters for each word, then submerged to get the next segment. The process took a good twenty minutes to complete. By the time Max rose to the top with the last letters of the coded message, Granny almost had the message completely solved. She took a few more minutes to decode the last word, then read the message aloud. She narrowed her eyes, her forehead creasing.

"What did you say was down there?" asked Granny.

"Percival drew every planet in our solar system, minus the moons, from Mars to Pluto. Though Pluto is now considered a dwarf planet because of its size."

Granny looked at the message again, then back up at Max.

"He wants us to pick one of these planets to open the door?" Granny was trying to rationalize it. It was interesting how Percival created a kind of security system to protect his valuables.

"I believe that's exactly what he wants us to do. Furthermore, he's giving us a clue here to do it. He wants us to narrow down which planet is not named after a god or goddess." Granny smiled knowingly.

"There is only one. _____!"

"Exactly!" Granny wrote down the answer and handed the notepad to Max. He slid the notepad and pen back into the plastic pouch and clipped it to his belt. Max and Granny swam back down to the wall. Max raised the spotlight and shined it on the wall while Granny raised her hand to one the planets, pressing her palm hard against the cold surface. To their right bubbles shot up. Granny and Max had to move back to a safe distance. They could see sunlight from above shining through the water. Though it appeared the water was shallow enough to allow light through above them, it was also deep enough to keep the lake floor dark and hidden, and getting deeper, as well as colder.

The rock slab had moved to cover the planets on the wall, allowing Granny and Max to swim past it into the lake. It didn't take long for the wall to close resolutely behind them. They could feel the thud of stone on stone. The only way they could go back now was if they swam to the surface and climbed back onto the island. That'd probably confuse the police.

Max shined the light down on the lake floor and noticed florescent arrows going out towards the back of the island. After glancing quickly at each other through the masks, Granny nodded and followed Max as he used the spotlight to guide them in the direction they needed to go.

TEN

AFTER AN HOUR, MAX WAS CERTAIN they were being led astray, swimming all over the lake in various depths of water, following arrows that didn't seem to be going anywhere. All they could see was sand, rocks, and plant life. Of course, fish were everywhere as well, big lurching predator fish and flashing schools of smaller ones.

Max was getting cold and tired. He would have been more concerned if they'd been fighting their way through fast currents or pounding surf. He'd have worried that their scuba tanks and bodies would give out, especially with Granny with him. But she was holding up just fine. This was not their first time scuba diving for either of them, so they were used to breathing the mixture of nitrogen and oxygen in the tank and were able to relax, which helped extend their time under water. Usually a tank for the average person lasted about eighty minutes. That could vary of course. Age had little to do with air consumption, so Granny wasn't in any more danger of running out of air in her tank than Max. It really depended a lot on fitness and experience, which suited Max and Granny well because they were both in shape and were experienced at diving.

Max followed the glow of the arrows until they led him straight to something unexpected. Near the opposite side of the lake, they came to a small brown chest tucked partially in the sand. Max could tell it had been there for months. On the front of the chest was a large lock. Feeling that the key they had found had something to do with it, Max removed it from around his neck and put it into the lock. He turned it forcefully. The lock opened. Max put the key back around his neck and lifted the lid of the chest. At first the chest looked empty, which was disappointing, but, as Max swam closer and looked directly inside he saw something. Lying in the bottom of the chest were several coins sealed in a clear plastic. The coins shone in the diffuse light and seemed to be in pristine condition.

Max showed Granny the coins before collecting them, holding them tightly within his fist. He then pointed up. Granny nodded and pushed off with her feet. When they reached the surface, Max removed his mouthpiece and lifted his mask from his eyes. He looked around them, seeing that the shore lay several yards away. Granny and Max swam to it. They were both deeply cold by now and needed to get out of the wetsuits fast. They took the time, though, to survey their surroundings. They hadn't realized just how far they had swum. Derwent Island seemed far away, and now other islands were nearer to where they stood.

After Max and Granny had stripped off the scuba tanks and wetsuits, they sat on the sand to rest. Max began to analyze the coins, trying to understand why they had to make that long swim to retrieve them. Before he could voice any opinion, a van pulled up. It was Reginald. He hopped out once he spied Granny.

"Are both of you all right?" Reginald's voice was filled with genuine concern as Granny and Max began to pick up their gear and backpacks.

"We're fine. How's Mia?" asked Max as he passed Reginald his wetsuit and tank and reached for Granny's. They stowed the gear in the back of the van. Max touched a button on his backpack to turn it back to normal. Granny did the same to hers.

"She's doing well, a little weak, but otherwise alive and well. The hospital's going to keep her under surveillance until tomorrow to make sure she has no reaction to the antidote Steven gave her, and to make sure the poison is fully out of her system. We'll be able to pick her up then. When I left her she was resting, so don't call her until later, Max. She wanted me to tell you that she'll be fine and that she loves you."

Max smiled, debating on contacting her. It took him a few minutes of inner turmoil, but decided to be patient and let her rest. He'd listen to Reginald and contact her later. He must think about what was best for Mia, not himself.

"How did you know we were here?" asked Granny as she climbed into the front seat to bask in the van's heat.

"I told him," spouted Morris.

Granny spun around to see both Morris and Steven in the back seat. "Not sure where you had gone, I was tracking you. Kind of a circuitous tour of the lake bottom, I take it. As soon as I realized that you were off the grounds, I rallied everyone."

Granny spotted the bruise upon Steven's cheek just as Max climbed into the back seat with the two boys.

"What happened to you?" Max asked.

Steven looked sheepish. Morris glanced his way.

Morris said, "Oh, it's nothing. Steven fell against something hard."

117

Neither Max nor Granny were fooled by this small lie.

Steven hissed, "Nasty things lies. They get you in trouble every time. You have to know they can see every one of them." Steven glared at Morris.

"I said I was sorry," Morris whined. "How many more times can I say it?"

"A few thousand more wouldn't hurt," said Steven, and he cracked a grin.

Morris, still sore about what had happened to Mia, looked away.

Max gave Morris a poke. "What's wrong with you? You've never acted like this before. What's going on?"

Morris shrugged. "Nothing! It's between Steven and me. I'm sorry for my outburst, it was . . . inappropriate." After a few moments of awkward silence, Morris added, "What did you find?"

Max stared at Morris several more moments before showing him the coins he held in his right hand. "We found these in a chest several yards off shore from here. They're Roman coins, if I'm not mistaken."

"Roman coins? What in the world would they be doing out there?"

Max shook his head.

"Steven, do you know anything about these?" asked Granny from the front seat as Reginald started up the van and pulled it back onto the road.

Steven glanced at Granny and shook his head. "Grandfather told me very little about them. What I do know is that you must figure out their significance in all this." Max sat back in his seat, rubbing his chin.

"Iron age settlers during Roman times came to certain parts of England for the extraction of iron ore," began Morris. "Coins, like these, were found in the Forest of Dean in 1848 by some workmen. There was a cavity in a group of rocks where three thousand Roman coins were found in earthenware jars in a special area known as Puzzlewood. No one knew why they were hidden there, but it did prove that the Romans had been in the area."

"The Forest of Dean is near Gloucester," offered Reginald.

Granny and Max's eyes lit up. Max snapped his fingers. "Many of the clues we found in the house were pointing us to Gloucester," he said. "The Richard the III information and the Beatrix Potter book. We figured out that the Panther must have lived in Gloucester at one time and if that's true, he might have a connection with the Forest of Dean and Puzzlewood. These coins were the last clue. Percival wants us to go to the Forest of Dean. Something must be hidden there he wants us to find, information that will reveal more about the Panther's true identity."

Reginald glanced at Granny. "To Puzzlewood, it is."

Granny nodded in agreement.

"You can let me off up here," said Steven. "I need to take care of some things. For now, my work is done." He sounded strangely confident.

"Are you sure you don't want to come with us?" asked Granny.

"I can't. My orders send me down another path. Besides, you've made it this far, I know you'll figure out the rest in no time. Don't worry, I'll see you soon enough."

Reginald pulled the van to a stop at the side of the road. Steven hurriedly said his good-byes and stepped out of the van.

Morris stepped partially out of the van and grabbed hold of Stevens' arm, stopping him. As Steven turned back, Morris's other hand flew swiftly to the collar of Steven's shirt before it slid down his shoulder to land on his upper arm. "Really, mate, I'm sorry about before. I hope there're no hard feelings between us. I know you were just doing your job, and I shouldn't have carried on so. I hope we can be friends?"

Morris smiled, his features and tone genuine.

Steven, at first cautious, soon overcame his suspicions. "Yeah, we can be friends. Good luck to you on your upcoming journey." Steven shook Morris's hand and pulled him close for a brief hug and slap on the back. When he let go, Morris popped back into the van and closed the door. Steven began his long walk down the road, not once looking back.

"Does that seem strange to anyone else?" asked Max as he glanced around the van. Morris stared at Steven through the window as he buckled his seatbelt.

"Very strange," said Morris, "but I'm sure Steven is on the next leg of his journey, whatever that may be. Remember, he's Percival's puppet. He'll do whatever his grandfather wants him to do." Morris's tone had a slight edge to it as he pulled out his laptop and began to type.

"I was talking about you and your strange behavior, actually." Max's eyes narrowed as he leaned towards Morris and turned the screen of his laptop towards him to take a look. Morris slammed a button with his pointer finger before glancing at Max. His screen revealed information about the Forest of Dean and Puzzlewood.

Morris sighed. "I'm sorry. I had an emotional day. For a few minutes I lost focus, but I'm fine now. Cut me some slack, mate. I'm not used to being in the field and experiencing all this first hand," Morris replied tersely.

Max pursed his lips as Morris's eyebrows raised. Max turned the screen back towards Morris before sitting back and shaking his head, focusing his mind on what was ahead. It had been an emotional day for all of them.

In the warmth of the van, both he and Granny began to relax and soon had fallen asleep. Both knew that they needed to recoup their energy and reserves. Sleep when they could was always a good plan.

ELEVEN

THE FOREST OF DEAN WAS A PLACE of varying landscapes. It became England's first National Forest Park in 1938 and was England's largest oak forest. Tucked between the rivers Leadon, Wye, and Severn in western Gloucestershire, the Forest of Dean was a few hour's drive away. It was vast and covered many acres. Morris thought their best bet was to start at Puzzlewood, located southwest of Gloucester. Reginald drove them to a town called Coleford, where they took a narrow road called the B4228 toward the town of Chepstow. About a half a mile they came to the entrance to Puzzlewood.

It was definitely a place for people to come and visit. Something about it seemed magical and appealing, almost luring them in. Puzzlewood was desolate at this time of year because of the cold. They saw no cars in the parking lot as they pulled in and parked. The team unloaded, putting on boots with metal grippers over the soles, providing them more secure footing. They weren't taking any chances on the slippery terrain.

"Where should we start?" asked Granny as she looked around and slipped her arms into the straps of her backpack.

"Let's start by following the path," suggested Reginald. "A slow jaunt in the tranquil woods is exactly what all of us needs to clear our minds. Look, the entrance is there." He pointed to a well-worn dirt track.

Max and Morris glanced at Reginald, who took Granny's hand and put it in the crook of his elbow and led the way. Before they even reached the sign at the head of the trail, a young woman emerged from a nearby building, the main office where visitors bought their tickets to get in. Since the tourist season had ended, they had thought they could just go in. They were mistaken.

"Wait!" the woman yelled as she waved her arm and came to a stop in front of them, her loose black hair flowing in the breeze while the steam from her breath filled the air. "You can't go in there. We're closed. Snow makes some of the trails slippery and dangerous. We can't afford to let you take risks, you see. So . . ." Before the woman could continue with what seemed a well-rehearsed speech, Reginald pulled out his badge, as did everyone else in the group, and showed the woman.

"We're detectives on a case. I assure you we've taken the proper precautions." Reginald tipped his foot for the woman to see what he meant.

The woman nodded as she scanned each badge thoroughly. She paused when she came to Max's. Her eyes instantly snapped up to his face. "You're Maxwell Sherlock Holmes? Is this the Crypto-Caper detective team?"

Max nodded. The woman stepped closer to Max, and slipped an envelope from the inside of her coat. "I've been hoping you'd come. I wanted to give this to you in person."

Max crinkled his forehead in confusion. He'd never met the woman before in his life. Then she whispered, "It's what you should be looking for."

Hesitantly, Max took the envelope from the woman's hands and thanked her. She backed away, breathing a sigh of relief. "Two men came here a few weeks ago. They were being very mysterious. We were just closing at that time, but they snuck in. I followed them, not wanting them to endanger themselves, and then I noticed what they were doing. I don't know exactly what these mean, but I thought you might. I heard them mention your name. The one guy said you'd be coming."

"Was one of the men older with crazy white hair?"

She looked amazed. "Yes, he looked like Albert Einstein."

Max turned his head slightly towards his team. "Percival was definitely here. I bet the other bloke was Steven."

Then the woman said, "Be forewarned. Please stay on the trails and be mindful of the cold and dustings of snow. One wrong step can send you falling into something you wish you hadn't."

As the woman walked away, Max opened the envelope. Tucked inside was a picture of rocks. They looked vaguely familiar, oddly shaped. They looked almost like a horse and a dragon. He recalled that, before they'd left on their adventure to the Lake District, they'd seen a picture of a horse and dragon on the back of Percival's letters written in ultraviolet ink. Back then they didn't know what it meant, but now it was starting to become clear. They were supposed to find them. He showed the rest of the group.

"What does this mean? It's rocks. Half this park is rocks," said Reginald as he stared at the pictures.

"Don't they look a little like a horse and dragon," Granny coached.

He twisted the photos around. "Well, maybe, but—"

Max took back the pictures. "We'll find out soon enough what all this means, I think."

The team began their descent into the woods. The further the team progressed the more impressed they were. Large pieces of rock were intermingling with the trees of the forest. Roots from ancient trees clung to some of the rocks causing quite an amazing effect. When the group came to a wooden bridge created from bound branches from trees, they paused. Max walked closer to the bridge and looked down below.

"What on earth are these kinds of rocks called? I've never seen anything like them before."

Morris glanced at his computer. "The Forest of Dean's iron ore deposits occur in features known as scowles, which are the surface expression of an eroding underground cave system. Uplift and erosion over the years eventually exposed this cave system, but that's what we're seeing. Puzzlewood is full of scowles of varying sizes. It's what causes the forest to look like a magical world. Scowles occur in a broken ring around the central part of the Forest of Dean and are confined to particular geological outcrops which consist of crease limestone, lower dolomite, drybrook limestone, and drybrook sandstone. The scowles were exploited by Iron Age settlers through to Roman times for their iron ore."

Max liked the strange configurations of stone as well as the moss that was draped over many of the scowles like a blanket.

They carefully crossed over the wooden bridge, which was surprisingly stable, and continued down the dirt path on the other side. The rule of thumb was to always stay on the paths, and at Puzzlewood, it was highly recommended. Straying from the path could find people quickly lost in the tangled wood. More important, it could cause damage to the surrounding area and the unique geologic features. The path was lined with small rocks and in certain areas had wooden fencing made of fallen branches and sticks that guided, and sometimes blocked, visitors.

The paths weaved throughout the woods, between scowles and up and down hills. Sometimes the path would go from dirt to rock. They periodically encountered rock steps as they descended lower into a valley, turning back to dirt on more level ground.

Max kept expecting the unusual trees to come alive and talk to him. The forest was that mysterious. Clouds filled the sky and a cool breeze sent a chill down their spines.

"We have been walking for an hour. Has anyone seen a horse or a dragon anywhere?" asked Granny.

"No, I don't believe so," answered Morris from the back of the line. Granny stopped and turned around, causing everyone else to do the same.

"Then what are we looking for exactly?" Max raised a hand to his chin.

"We're searching for rocks or a formation or something in the shape of a horse or dragon. I don't know exactly where we're going to find it, but it looks like these scowles should be in the shape of them. I've imagined bunnies, a cat, three stouts, and a wild boar, but nothing close to a horse or dragon." Granny turned to Reginald, when she spotted something. The path ahead led them through several more scowles. What caught her attention was formations that seemed to be in the shape of a dragon's mouth. "Let me see that picture again."

Max pulled out the envelope and took out the picture, handing it to Granny. "Of course—finally. Look! There's our dragon." As Granny pointed, everyone noticed the same features about the rocks and rushed over to them.

"Everyone, look carefully at the rocks. See if there's a hidden recess somewhere, a small enough hole to fit a hand in." The group dispersed and began their search, combing every single part of the scowle. Morris, his laptop in his backpack, began searching along with everyone else. Not seeing anything out of the ordinary, he used his hands to caress and inspect the rocks in front of him.

Morris looked up and noticed that Granny and Reginald were standing off to the side. Max joined them. Morris called, "I found nothing. You?"

"Nothing!" said Granny.

Reginald shook his head. Morris was about to lower his hands, also claiming defeat, when he noticed a shadowy spot in a crease of rock. It looked darker than the surrounding rock. Morris slowly touched the spot. He soon realized it was a hole. He quickly took out his flashlight and aimed the beam into the space.

"I think I found something," he exclaimed with excitement, surprised at his discovery.

Granny, Max, and Reginald huddled around Morris as he reached into the hole. He carefully felt around. Most of what his fingers touched was just damp rock. But not everything. After a few seconds he withdrew his hand, holding a piece of paper between his finger tips. Without even looking at it, he handed it to Max.

Max hastily opened the folds. On the front of the paper was a picture of a dragon, looking similar to the image Percival had drawn on the back of his letters with ultraviolet ink. There were also a series of numbers on the back, but instead of groups of three numbers in the Ottendorf cipher, there were only two.

1-34   3-24
2-12   4-25
3-4   4-32

"What are these numbers for?" asked Reginald.

"I think they're for a book cipher," answered Max.

"Shouldn't there be three numbers?" inquired Morris. "Like the ones Mia had solved?"

"I-I don't know!" stuttered Max.

"Do we have the book or something to decode it?" included Granny.

"Hold up!" Max shouted. "I'm not Mia. I don't know a whole lot about these ciphers."

"Just relax and think!" encouraged Granny as she patted Max's back.

"Let's keep moving forward. Hopefully, more information will reveal itself shortly. We still need to find the horse."

Max held onto the paper and led the way further down the trail. Off to their right, in an out-of-the-way spot, was a rock with several trees and roots coming out of its top. The group stopped and stared. It looked for all the world like a horse. The foursome walked over and began searching the scowles. This time it was Granny who had found the hidden recess. Inside was also a piece of paper. Max opened it and stared at the image of a horse similar, again, to the picture drawn by Percival in ultraviolet ink. Below it was another series of numbers.

1-7	3-35
1-12	4-4
3-12	4-12
3-17	5-17
3-26	

"More numbers for the cipher?" asked Reginald.

Max thought about the connections between everything. "I think I have an idea. Let's find our way back to the van. We can warm up and maybe figure this out."

The return trip to the parking lot took the group another hour and a half. Once inside, Reginald cranked the heat as they sat and thawed. Max pulled out the pictures they'd been given and the letters they'd found while Morris pulled out his laptop. Reginald and Granny turned anxiously in their seats to watch what evolved. Max stared at the numbers and the pictures for some time.

"Mia said something before we left for this case. She wondered if there was a motif of a horse and dragon on the Globe Theater gates. At the time, we didn't understand how they fit in, but I think I know. In Percival's house there was a book of Shakespeare's works. Mia didn't choose it. She chose the Beatrix Potter book instead and we found the key to open the chest on the bottom of the lake. But because she chose the Beatrix Potter book doesn't mean that she didn't also want to choose the Shakespeare book. I think she wanted them both, feeling they had equal importance. It was a trick. Morris, you said you pulled up a key to the images on the Bankside Gates, to the location of the motifs."

"Yes! I have two views. One is from the gate by the front of the Globe Theatre, and the other is the view from the Thames.

Why?" Before Max could answer, Morris's eyes and features registered his understanding. "I know why. You want me to look at the key and see if there are motifs of a horse and a dragon on there. Well, let's take a look." Morris's fingers worked quickly as he pulled up the picture on his screen. He then adjusted his screen so everyone could see it.

"The front gates are labeled from 1 to 63. The back gates are labeled from 64 to 125. Each motif was taken from some animal or item talked about in Shakespeare's plays. On the front side of the gate we see a horse—motif 24. And looky here, it was taken from *Richard III* from part V, scene IV." Morris worked his magic as he pulled up a book of all of Shakespeare's plays. It was a collection of sorts. Morris typed in the part and the scene number. The book appeared to come to life. It opened its pages, moving swiftly as it stopped to the required page. Morris read the lines until he came to the part that contained the information they were looking for. He read the following:

"Slave, I have set my life upon a cast,
And I will stand the hazard of the die:
I think there be six Richmond's in the field;
Five have I slain to-day instead of him.
A horse! A horse! My kingdom for a horse!"

"Now what?" asked Granny.

"We use the series of numbers to decode the hidden message. The reason why there are only two numbers and not three, is because there is no page number. There are dozens of different copies available of Shakespeare's works. All we are supposed to do is find the line and the letter on that line. For example," said Max. "The first number in the series is 1-7. We use the first line and look at the seventh letter on that line. That would be the letter 'H.' The next one is 1-12, which equals the letter 'E.' Granny, could you write these down please?" Max removed Mia's notepad from his backpack and handed it to Granny.

"Ready?" Once Max saw Granny's head nod, he continued. "3-12 equals 'B.' 3-17 is an 'R.' 3-25 is 'I.' 3-35 is 'D.' 4-4 is 'E.' 4-12 is 'A.' Then lastly, 5-17 equals 'N.'

1-7=H	3-35=D
1-12=E	4-4=E
3-12=B	4-12=A
3-17=R	5-17=N
3-26=I	

So, we have the word 'Hebridean.'" Max scrutinized the word for several seconds and looked at Morris. "Hebridean?"

Morris looked up the word. Once he clicked on the information, he raised his hand to his mouth. "It's not Hebridean. The word can also mean 'The Hybrides'. The Hybrides, also known as Fingal's Cave, is a famous overture written by Felix Mendelssohn while residing on these islands. The Hebrides have a diverse geology ranging in age from Precambrian strata that are amongst the oldest rocks in Europe to Tertiary igneous intrusions. The Hebrides can be divided into two main groups, separated from one another by The Minch to the north and the Sea of the Hebrides to the south. The Inner Hebrides lie closer to mainland Scotland and include Staffa and the Small Isles. There are thirty-six inhabited islands in this group." Morris ran his hands through his hair after he read the sentences.

"Which island are we talking about specifically?" inquired Granny.

"There are thirty-six possibilities?"

"Yes, but only one island has Fingal's Cave on it."

Max glanced at the other series of numbers for the dragon picture. "Morris, where's the dragon motif found on the gate?"

Morris maneuvered around pages until he reached the one for the back gate. "It is the 122 motif, and found also in *Richard III*. It can be found in part V, scene III." Morris typed in the corresponding numbers in his on-line Shakespeare book. It turned to the following section. Once Morris found the sentences pertaining to the information of the dragon, he read them aloud.

"A thousand hearts are great within my bosom:
Advance our standards, set upon our foes
Our ancient word of courage, fair Saint George,
Inspire us with the spleen of fiery dragons!
Upon them! Victory sits on our helms."

Max wrote down the letters next to each number series.

1-34=S	3-24=F
2-12=T	4-25=F
3-4=A	4-32=A

The word 'Staffa' stood out. And Max knew what that meant. "It's the island of Staffa that Fingal's Cave's on. That should be our next course."

Reginald screwed up his face. "The island's off the coast of Scotland. We're going to have to fly there. It'd take us too long to drive."

"There's an airport not far from Mia. If she's okay, let's pick her up and take her with us. She'd appreciate it and is probably dying to learn what we have found out," stated Max.

The others agreed, and they headed back towards the Lake District. They decided they'd check into a hotel for the night after they reached Mia and before their journey to Staffa the following morning. They could all use a good meal and some serious rest.

TWELVE

DRIVING BACK TO THE LAKE DISTRICT took hours, and felt never-ending. Everyone was exhausted from their chilly walk through the Forest of Dean. It was no surprise when Max, Morris, and Granny all fell asleep while Reginald drove nonstop towards Mia. It was dark by the time he pulled the van into the Derwent hospital, a small place barely more than a clinic. Everyone woke up as soon as they felt the van stop. After getting their bearings, the group walked into the hospital. They immediately headed to room five where Mia had been registered, but when they walked into the room, the bed was empty. A nurse was straightening it.

"Excuse me, but where is Mia Holmes? Did you change her room?"

The nurse narrowed her eyes. "No, she was released a few hours ago by her grandfather and brother."

Max narrowed his eyes. Granny gasped and stiffened, wondering if Harold had finally revealed himself.

"I'm her brother, and I obviously didn't pick her up. My grandfather's dead, so I don't believe he did either."

Confusion filled the nurse's features. "Well, I . . . I . . . I just don't know what to say. They had IDs and Mia did go with them willingly . . . so . . ."

"Where is your sign out log?" demanded Granny. "Someone had to sign her out. I want to see who."

"Our patients' privacy is important, ma'am. I just can't give out their information without proof that . . ." Before the nurse could continue, Reginald and Granny pulled out their badges.

"I don't believe I was asking you," Granny said. "Your sign out log. Now, please."

The nurse, looking annoyed examined the badges. She then exhaled loudly. She gave a brief nod and led the way to the front desk. She picked up the clipboard with the sign out log.

"Right here. See? A man named Percival Peacock signed her out. Isn't that the grandfather?"

Max looked at Granny, whom he saw physically relax. She looked relieved. "No, not that I am aware of, and I'd know," sassed Granny.

"We've been played," admitted Max, smacking a fist into his other palm. "I'm really getting frustrated now." He hit the counter.

The nurse behind the counter jumped, Max gave her a sympathetic glance of apology. The action seemed to wake the nurse up because she then looked at something lying next to her. The nurse grabbed it and handed it to the nurse with the clipboard. The nurse looked at the small manila envelope. She held it out to Granny. "Is this you?"

Granny grabbed the envelope and looked at her name penned nicely on the front. Morris grabbed Max's arm with one hand and tugged on the back of Granny's coat with the other.

"Thank you, ma'am. We appreciate your help." They left the hospital and piled back into the van. Max and Granny turned to Morris, eager to know why he had pulled them out.

"What? We have to figure out where Percival and Steven took Mia," blurted Max. "Why were you so eager to leave?"

Morris shrugged. "We already know where. Percival and Steven have taken Mia to Staffa, and I bet the envelope we just received will confirm it. Granny, if I may?"

Granny handed Morris the envelope. Everyone in the van watched as Morris opened the envelope and pulled out a CD. Morris opened the CD player on his laptop and placed the disc inside. Soon the music began to flow throughout the van.

"What composer are we listening too?" asked Reginald of no one in particular.

"We're listening to German composer Felix Mendelssohn. This is his *Hebrides Overture Opus 26*, I believe." Morris smiled. "It's one of Mia's personal favorites. I've heard her listening to it before. It's also known as his Fingal's Cave overture. This confirms that we're going to Fingal's Cave off the coast of Scotland." He grinned more widely. "It also means we solved all the clues for the dragon and horse correctly. Percival wants us to meet him there. With all of the other information we acquired, we know that's exactly what he wants us to do." Morris took the CD from his laptop. "If it makes any of you feel better, I can tell you exactly where they are now."

Max, Granny and Reginald stared at Morris in confusion, then Max smiled. "That's why you were so sweet to Steven. I knew you were too angry to get over it that fast. You were up to something. You tagged him with a tracking device didn't you?" Max clucked his tongue and shook his head while Morris pressed a few buttons on his laptop. "We're rubbing off on you, mate. You have to admit it."

"I'll admit nothing. Look, they're already in Scotland and staying at an inn near the Glascow airport. Mia's GPS is working. Right next to her is Steven. See the blue dot?" Max nodded as he glanced at the screen.

"How is she doing?"

"Her heart beat is up a bit, which could mean she's under duress. All her other vitals are normal. There's no poison in her system, which is a relief."

"What do you think Percival wants with Mia? Other than the obvious, of course," stated Granny.

"I can think of a few reasons why he'd come out of hiding to get her. What's irking me the most is that this may not have been about the Panther entirely. Mia appears to be a pawn in all of this. I think she was Percival's main target. He sent us on his scavenger hunt, distracting us from what he was going to do. We need to get to him, and fast."

"There's an airport nearby where Scotland Yard keeps a jet. I'll make a few calls and see that it's ready for our departure tomorrow morning." Max was the first one to jump on Reginald's words.

"Tomorrow morning? No, that's too late."

"We need to act now," added Morris.

"It'll do Mia no good if we're too tired to function. In the dark we won't be able to see the surprises Percival may have in store for us. We need to rest and have a good meal, because I don't know about you, but I'm starving and tired."

Max and Morris could hear the rumbling of their own stomachs, feeling the ache of hunger. Granny agreed with Reginald's idea and squashed any other objections.

THIRTEEN

THE SKY WAS AS GLOOMY AND DARK IN SCOTLAND as was the Crypto-Capers moods. They had left early that morning to fly to the Glasgow International Airport in Scotland. From there they took a taxi to the Paisley Gilmour Street Station where they hopped on a train that headed to Oban. The option of driving was out, for it would have taken them nearly two hours to get there. Train was faster. Though the scenery was beautiful, Morris and Max were too distracted to enjoy the view.

Max sat quietly pouring over clues and information they had gathered from the very beginning of the case, while Morris was on his laptop checking on Mia's status and looking up other things. Granny watched both of them. Though her features appeared calm, her mind was racing a mile a minute.

When the train pulled into the station at Oban, the team unloaded and headed to the Caledonia-MacBrayne ferry which crossed to the Isle of Mull in about an hour and ran several times each day, all year long. When they reached the Isle of Mull, the team took a bus to Fionnphort, where the boat that would take them on the next leg of their journey, around the island of Staffa. When they finally reached the boat, the team was worn out from all of their traveling. The journey had taken them most of the day.

But as the boat set off from the dock and headed towards the island, hope began to fill their chests.

"What do we know about the island?" asked Max as he glanced at Morris, knowing full well that he had been doing research on the island and the cave.

"Staffa's uninhabited. Only animals visit, including the puffin. Fingal's Cave was formed entirely from hexagonally-jointed basalt columns, similar in structure to the Giant's Causeway in Northern Ireland, and those of nearby Ulva. They were all created by an ancient lava flow. When the lava began to cool, the surface cracked in characteristic hexagonal pattern in a similar way that mud cracks and shrinks when it dries. The cracks gradually extended down into the mass of lava, cooling, then shrinking to form columns, which were then exposed to erosion from the elements. As you can see and feel, there are many elements at work here."

The wind had begun to pick up, causing the frigid water around the boat to rise up and splash them repeatedly.

They were coming up on the cave. All eyes seemed to focus on the opening. It was such an oddity of nature, and it was amazing to behold. The cave had a large arched entrance filled by the sea. The base had to have been around twenty meters wide and eighty meters deep. The captain told them that they would not be able to go inside of the cave. The closer the boat approached the cave the louder an eerie sound filled the air. Granny glanced at Reginald, then Max and Morris, her eyes narrowing as she focused more intently on the sound.

The rough waves pounded the wall of the cave, giving it an atmosphere of a natural cathedral. It was also known as the cave

of melody. They could hear why. The waves caused an echoing inside of the cave, not unlike an orchestra playing. Max could understand why Felix Mendelssohn created his overture from it. It was purely amazing and hard to describe. It exceeded all their expectations. Morris glanced around wondering when they were going to meet up with Percival—he soon found out.

The group noticed another boat coming towards them from their left. All eyes focused on the boat until it was upon them. Then, with a last big splash, the boat stopped right beside them. A man, with crazy white hair, waved at them.

"Come aboard!" the man commanded. As the others began to move forward, the man pointed a rough finger at Reginald. "You . . . you may stay behind. Your services are not required."

"I'm a part of this team. I'll be joining them wherever they're going."

140

Percival frowned. In a harsher voice, he sneered, "You, sir, *will* stay behind, or I'll leave and this whole effort will all be for nothing." When a response didn't come immediately, Percival turned the wheel, and the boat veered away.

"No!" Max shouted, prompting Reginald's response.

"All right!" shouted Reginald. "I'll stay behind. Just bring them back to me when you're finished. I'll be waiting. And God help you if your intentions for them is of the devious kind."

The man revealed a thin smile. He backed up the boat and waited until Max, Morris, and Granny grabbed their backpacks and boarded. He then nodded his head and winked. As soon as everyone was situated, the man had turned the boat quickly and hit the gas. The engine propelled them forward towards the other side of the island. Granny could see Reginald throwing his belongings to the bottom of the boat in a fit of frustration. Soon, he was a dot in the distance.

When they arrived at their destination, the man turned off the engine and dropped anchor. For several minutes they drifted, all eyes on Percival, who was calm as the sheltered water, yet in his depths was a hidden storm. He reached into his pocket and pulled out a black cap to cover his hair. He was wearing a long black coat with matching gloves.

"Percival Peacock, I presume?" asked Max.

The man smiled. "Yes, I am Percival Peacock. And you, my friends, are the Crypto-Capers team, minus one. It's a pleasure to finally meet you. I've been waiting for some time for this pleasure, as you can imagine." Percival licked his lips in excitement, then he added impatiently, "Let's dispense with the formalities. I see you found the clues I laid out for you. Please, while we are in this desolate place undisturbed, tell me what you know about the Panther."

Max and Morris glanced at each other. Morris nodded and Max turned to face Percival, beginning the tale.

"First, we received your letter that led us to the Globe Theatre. We knew the theatre was created in honor of William Shakespeare's works. The Panther's history begins in the theater. His first play was called *After the Taming of the Shrew*, which was first performed, ironically, in the Globe Theatre. William Shakespeare and Moliere were his favorite playwrights, combining their style with his own. *After the Taming of the Shrew* was his very first big hit, which thrust him into the world of theater and ignited his passion for it. This explains why he was working in Las Vegas for so long trying to get his various plays off the ground. He was undercover with the identity of Julian Cross. He blended in. Had a fiancé. Had an almost normal life, until Denton tried to steal that antique sock in Florida where this all began, ruining everything for him.

"Let's picture that. The illustrious Panther hiding from society in plain sight, but his son suddenly arrives, finds him, and needs his help. The Panther is then forced to deal with his son's serious dilemma without revealing himself. He was blowing his cover. After exhausting all resources, he had no choice but to come out of hiding. He lures us into his Red Rock Canyon hideout, revealing to us who he really was in the end. That situation makes him resent his son, which is why he's been throwing him in harm's way ever since. But Denton's skills improved since Florida. We found that out in Pisa, which means that the Panther felt pity for his son and has been teaching him his secret ways, probably because he has no other heir.

"By leaving us clues, like the Shakespeare motifs on the gates at the Globe Theatre, we were able to deduce that the Panther lived in Gloucester near the Forest of Dean. His father was some type of tailor, and I feel that he has some anger towards an absent mother. In Denton's case, I feel the Panther's anger is for an absent wife. The woods often interested him. He hid from his past there, which was why you sent us to the Forest of Dean in the first place where we saw the pictures made of rock and wood of the horse and the dragon. You wanted us to discover how the Panther visualized things. I'll admit, the Panther is a genius in his own right. I respect him greatly, yet despise him at the same time."

Max paused, waiting for approval. The smile on Percival's face showed that he was correct.

"You're an impressive youth, Maxwell. There's no doubt about that. You absorbed and uncovered more than even I knew. But let me correct you on one point, disclosing some information I know you do not possess." Percival paused briefly. "The Panther does have another heir." Max looked intently at Percival.

"Who?"

"He has a daughter, who is older than Denton. Her name's Elora. She was born when the Panther was a much younger man, at the very beginning of his career, in fact. She's disavowed her relationship with him, forcing him out of her life. Periodically, he tries to contact her. But she refuses to speak with him. She's embarrassed at what he has become. He's changed so much over the years. Her mother, Jacqueline, passed away many years ago. She was caught in the cross fire between the police and the Panther. Jacqueline was trying to explain, to defend him, because his first crime was out of necessity—they were poor. The police would not listen. Because of that, she was the first causality. It broke the Panther's heart, turning him in such a way that he had become cold and calculating, evil and elusive. It started the transition to the man he is today."

Percival's words made sense to the Crypto-Caper team. But it also left more unanswered questions.

"You mentioned in your letter we found in the Globe Theatre that the Panther was an excellent student. Who taught him his cunning ways?" inquired Max.

Percival took a deep breath. "You must understand that the legend of the Panther has been around longer than the man. The current Panther was taught the tricks of the trade, and the secrets of being so elusive, by a man named Marburrow. Marburrow was the original Panther. Getting older, he decided he wanted to retire. He was more than happy to let the legend of the Panther disappear along with him, but then he ran across our emotionally destroyed friend in a pub one night. Marburrow saw the perfect opportunity to train a successor to take his place so he could be left alone to live a life of luxury. The current Panther has held this position of infamy for a number of years. There's a good chance he'll pass down the legacy to Denton, and if not to him, then someone else."

Percival's words made everyone think for a good five minutes.

"What happened to the original Panther?" asked Morris.

"His life ended in an ironic twist of fate. He was in the Caribbean, living that life of leisure fishing he desired, when he fell overboard and was attacked by a shark."

Morris cringed in response.

Granny had another question. "Percival," she crooned gently. "How do you know the Panther has another heir? By the tone in your voice when you mentioned Elora's name, I believe she's close to you in some way."

Percival smiled at Granny. "The degree to which your whole team is observant, I should've been more careful. So be it. Yes, I'm close to her. Elora's married to my youngest son, Drake. I love her like a daughter, and she treats me like her father. They've been married for a few years now and have a beautiful daughter named Jocelyn. They're in hiding. Since the Panther began his attack on my life, I told them to leave their estate and go on holiday somewhere. They're well protected, I assure you."

"I know what you did," said Morris accusingly, his eyes narrowing. "You're distracting the Panther's attention away from you and your family by giving him another target to focus on. What target did you give him?"

All eyes were turned to Percival. "One he was already intending to acquire. I just created the opportunity for him sooner."

"Meaning?" demanded Max, glancing around the boat cautiously, fearing the Panther was going to drive up in another boat and capture them. They were certainly easy pickings, but it wasn't the case at all. Then it dawned on him.

"Where's Mia?"

Percival said nothing, his eyes averted. "Would you be so callous and desperate as to give my sister to that evil traitor?"

Percival's head shot up. "Absolutely not! No, I would never do that. I need her help. In fact, I need all of your talents." Percival pulled out a large blue-and-purple book which had a peacock feather tucked through it. He handed it to Granny. "Here is one of the Peacock Diaries. Give it to your man waiting for you back at the boat. He works for Scotland Yard, doesn't he?" The slight pause gave him his answer. "Have him take it back to his superiors. They will be pleased with the information within. They will also leave me alone and the case will be closed."

"Do you think it will be that easy?" asked Granny, fearing that it wouldn't be.

"Yes, I do, and I will tell you why it will be that simple. Once they look at the information inside of the diary, they'll have no more use for me. It'll also keep them busy for weeks to come." The mysteriousness of Percival intrigued them all. Then he said something unpredictable. "I've been thinking about it for some time, and I would like to help your team. In fact, I want to become your new backer. There are lots of crimes out there that need your special talents to solve. I want to help, and in the process, we'll eventually capture the Panther together."

Max, Morris and Granny all glanced at each other.

"Why don't you just reveal his name and we can forget about the whole ordeal," spouted Morris logically.

"I can't do that. Revealing his name will reveal his daughter's existence and will put her life at risk. You already know that Denton's last name is not Miles. He'd changed it for the same reason that Elora changed hers. But Denton has soiled his new name, Elora hasn't. I refuse to put her into harm's way. Despite what the Panther has become, his daughter is as sweet as a morning flower. She's a very kind and unselfish woman. I will not drag her through the mud along with her father, because once his name is revealed, the world will come after her to get to him.

"Believe me when I say that will be exactly what happens. They'll find her birth certificate, and in so doing, will reveal much more than what is needed. The world will exploit her."

146

"Who exactly was Jacqueline?" questioned Max, having a feeling that Jacqueline's history was also a contributor to the problem. She was someone important, though Percival was not directly saying it.

Percival smirked as he ignored Max's remark, proceeding to plead his case with Granny. "Nellie, you have enough experience in this world to know I speak the truth. Any group with enough power would draw attention to Elora and endanger my son and their daughter's safety."

Granny slowly nodded, knowing full well that Percival spoke the truth. She also remembered her conversation with Chief Inspector Jaffrey and how he had dwelled on the idea himself.

"So, let me get this straight. You want to finance us?" interrupted Max.

"Not just finance, my dear boy, but provide you with the things you need, like jets to fly you wherever you want to go somewhere, not this fiddling around with tickets at airports. I could also provide you with new equipment to help you. Morris has been doing a grand job, but I feel I can add something to the team. I'll be behind the scenes, filtering the good jobs from the bad. In all honesty, I see aspiring detectives who will one day be famous. I want you to become legend. There're no strings attached, I promise."

Max was unsure of what Percival was offering.

Granny understood completely. "We'll discuss this as a team, Percival. You make a very generous offer."

"Yes, I do. Well, while you think about it, here is something for you to ponder on as well." Percival removed a manila envelope from his inside coat pocket and handed it to Max. "Don't look at it until you've finished your business with Scotland Yard. I guarantee you'll be interested in the Panther's next target."

"And Mia? Where is she?" persisted Max again.

"She'll be with me. I need her expertise on something. Don't worry. You'll be joining her in a week or so when things blow over. I'll send a private jet to pick you up. I suggest you be on it. A coded letter will arrive giving you instruction."

"Wait a minute," began Granny, raising her hand.

"No, there's no more waiting. We're out of time." Percival started the boat and whipped it around, causing the team to lose their balance and pile up on the other side of the boat. It didn't take them long to return to where Reginald was waiting for them. His arms were folded across his chest and a scowl was set upon his features. Before they were within earshot, Percival reminded the team of what he'd said. When the boat stopped alongside the other one, he watched them unload and board the other vessel. Then, he took off just as quickly, sprays of water spouting up behind him.

"What happened?" demanded Reginald. "What was said?"

Granny handed Reginald the diary. "This is for you. Take it! It'll reveal the truth that your brother and the Yard are looking for. Percival is going to go back into hiding."

Reginald took the diary and held it tightly to his chest. Morris sat down on a seat and pulled out his laptop, typing in some information while Max sat lost in thought, feeling the motion of the boat as it began to move forward away from the island.

FOURTEEN

DAYS LATER, AFTER THEIR RETURN TO LONDON, the Crypto-Caper team had finished their debriefing with Scotland Yard. The business with Percival Peacock was over. The case was closed. Percival had been right. The diary was like fresh chum in an ocean of hungry sharks. In the days to come, there were several arrests. News was plastered all over the radio and television almost every second of the day. Some high ranking officials and lords had been arrested for an assortment of crimes dealing on various levels of corruption. Percival had given them some very important information in the Peacock Diary. It was exactly what Chief Inspector Jaffrey was looking for. He told them that for years there had been speculation about who the bad apples were in parliament and in Scotland Yard, but of course there was no proof—until now. There were even pictures and videos of the persons committing the acts. The evidence was irrefutable.

Morris received news from his contacts in Australia. They confirmed Asher's story. Asher Montgomery had been recruited by the Panther to do a job, but he was an unwilling accomplice. His sister, Ria, had been found in Victoria by Morris's friends and released from the Panther's care, thus free Asher from the Panther's control. The Panther had escaped from the police and was on the run. Morris was tracking him through his computer and found him somewhere in the Mediterranean on a ship, his destination unknown.

The Crypto-Capers were satisfied with the ending of the case, receiving much praise from Scotland Yard, but they were left waiting for news from Percival about Mia's location. Morris had been tracking her, but her exact location remained unclear. Something was disrupting the connection. To make matters worse, Max and Mia's parents were off the grid. News of them returning home was now a memory with assurances that as soon as something was found out about their disappearances they would be notified immediately. To say emotions at the Holmes' residence ran high was an understatement.

The manila envelope that Percival had given them contained maps of Europe, along with some pictures of various items, including a decorative egg. Not really knowing what was going on, everything they looked at was left for speculation. In the envelope was also a flash drive. A note with it said not to run the flash drive until they were contacted and that Percival would know if they did. Morris's fingers were getting itchy. He wanted to dive right into the information, but he restrained himself.

Max was pacing the floors, while Granny was trying to master her knitting, trying to relax, though Max and Morris saw the tangled mass thrown several times across the room. Then it happened. The door bell rang. The trio all moved from their locations and crowded at the door. Granny expertly bumped the boys with her hips, and reached the door first. She straightened her hair, smoothed her dress, then opened the door. Their security man stood there, holding an envelope.

"This just came for you by private messenger, Nellie. I've already checked it and it has been cleared." He then handed Granny the envelope."

"Thank you, Gracin. I appreciate it."

"A black sedan is also waiting for you and your team out front. The driver says that Percival Peacock is offering you his services? If you do not agree with this, I'll handle it and remove the vehicle straight away."

Granny shook her head. "No, we're expecting him. Thanks, Gracin."

The man nodded and disappeared through a secret corridor in the hallway, talking into a radio pinned to his shoulder. Granny closed the door and looked at the rest of the group. Max and Morris both looked anxious. Granny gently opened the envelope and removed a piece of paper. On it was a cryptogram.

A H X R H X   G W E I H E C .

C K W E C O   U W X B C Q M .

I E W T G C Q   G W E D G O .
9 4 2 3

"Max!" Granny whispered urgently as she handed him the message. Max hurried across the room to where Mia's notebook lay on a coffee table and opened it. Once he saw the cipher key he had used for the other cryptograms, he immediately placed the message by it and filled it in. He then read it aloud.

"Let's go!" spouted Morris as he turned and headed for their bags, which they had kept packed and ready for this moment. Granny was the only one standing still.

"What are you doing?" asked Max as he placed his hand upon Granny's arm.

"Can we trust Percival? I'm starting to doubt this whole situation. What are we getting ourselves into, Max?"

Max looked at her. Her eyes were tearful as they held fast to his. "We must go, must face this—whatever it is. We have to find Mia and bring her home. We must do what we can, and I almost regretfully have to say, join forces with Percival. He's a man of means and connection. He knows way more than we do about what's in the mind of the Panther and what's going on. Percival will guide us to where we need to go. He'll help us catch the Panther. It seems that he's devoted to it as much as we are."

After several minutes, Granny nodded and turned to Morris. "Morris, I don't care what Percival says, run the drive. We need to know what we're up against. I can't get into that car and leave here without knowing."

Morris needed no coaxing. He hastily plugged in the flash drive and ran it. Morris typed rapidly on the keyboard as he bypassed every security feature that tried to prevent him from accessing it. After several minutes, Morris broke through the security wall revealing at least a dozen pictures.

The team stared at the pictures in disbelief. Each picture was of them in a place they had already been. There was a picture of them in Florida, Las Vegas, the Riviera Maya, Italy, and of course, the Lake District and Staffa. No one knew what to say. Even Max was speechless. Then some new pictures sprang up from a location they haven't been. They saw the tear drop towers of the Kremlin and knew it was Russia. Granny was about to open her mouth to speak when another picture filled the screen. She gasped as her hand rose to her mouth. Mitchem and Martha Holmes, Max and Mia's parents, were in the picture. They were handcuffed with hands behind their backs. They were in a type of jail cell surrounded by what looked like the Russian police.

"Oh, no!" wheezed Granny as her hand lowered to her chest. "If the Russian police have them in custody, they're in trouble."

"Granny," Max tried to think rationally. "We don't know if their identities have been compromised. Just breathe!"

Granny regained her composure until she saw a picture of another man. He appeared older, yet his hair was black. He had a full beard and a mustache. Max didn't recognize him. The pictures caught the man talking with the Panther in Australia. They could see the opera house in the background. The men shook hands and hugged, as if they were close friends. Max studied each scene as it unfolded. When the men parted, they had smiles of their faces, but when the man with the black hair walked away, the picture was of his features as he glanced back. The smile was replaced by a look of disgust, then one of deceit, Max was sure of it. This man was not cooperating with the Panther out of free choice. He, too, was being coerced. It was then he noticed the man's eyes, and they seemed familiar.

Max couldn't place them, but Granny could. Her intake of breath caused Morris and Max to turn. As they watched, she seemed to topple, fold up onto herself. They rushed toward her, but she fainted and hit the ground with a loud THUD!

"Granny, are you all right? Granny!" Max shouted as he tapped her cheeks. Granny's eyes opened and fluttered quickly as she shook her head.

"What is it Granny?" inquired Morris as he snapped his fingers to get her attention. Her eyes soon focused on his for only a few seconds.

Granny took a deep, ragged breath and pushed herself into a sitting position.

"What is it?" Max asked again.

In a somewhat thin voice, Granny wheezed, "It's true! He's alive. Harold's alive!"

THE END

Look for the next adventure in Book 6 of the Crypto-Capers series:

ETH CRUICS OFR IERH